Christmas in Havenport

Ruth A. Casie

Lita Harris

Emma Kaye

Nicole S. Patrick

Timeless Scribes
Publishing

Timeless Scribes Publishing LLC

Print   ISBN-10: 1-945679-07-7
         ISBN-13: 978-1-945679-07-0

Digital ISBN-10: 1-945679-08-5
         ISBN-13: 978-1-945679-08-7

Cover created by Jay Aheer at Simply Defined Art
Edited by One More Time Editing, LLC
Copy Edited by One More Time Editing, LLC

This edition published by arrangement with Timeless Scribes
Publishing LLC.

www.TimelessScribes.com

Havenport Herald

*** Winter Edition ***   *** Premier Issue ***

Get the latest with Candy Apples.
Gossip with a snarky, tart bite…

GET READY FOR SNOW!

Seems like The Final Chapter bookstore is the place to be this Christmas. As the snow piles up, customers are hooking up left and right just in time for a little holiday cheer. Does this reporter's heart good to see it.

❄ ❄ ❄

Havenport's favorite romantic comedy author said **I'll Be Home for Christmas** and she's made good on her word. Despite some rather nasty reviews on her new book, she'll be at The Final Chapter signing alongside the thriller writer we've all been drooling over lately. These two have been heating up the web with their rivalry and I can't wait to see the sparks fly in person. Something tells me our gal's in for a bit of a shock when she realizes the handsome hunk she was seen flirting with is actually her arch nemesis.

❄ ❄ ❄

It's with a sad heart that I announce The Final Chapter bookstore will soon be closing its doors. But maybe there's still hope? The owner's niece seems to be at a crossroads and has shown interest in taking over the store. Lets hope the strong, silent-type newcomer she's been seen cozying up to on the beach can convince her to take a chance and make a new life in this **Winter Wonderland** we call home.

❄ ❄ ❄

Our Havenport Elementary School art teacher shocked the ladies at The Final Chapter book signing by reading a spell to "bring forth true love." Is it a coincidence a hottie dressed like a nineteenth century sailor showed up that same night? He may be giving her a bit of a cold shoulder now, but let's hope he warms up soon, because **Baby, It's Cold Outside**. (And just in case that spell really worked, I need a copy of that book, please.)

❄ ❄ ❄

Please tell me someone snapped a picture of that little Scottish Terror, uh Terrier, we all know and avoid peeing on Havenport's car repairman extraordinaire. (Email all pics to Candy Apples via The Havenport Herald). I'll grant the former Marine had a right to be peeved, but my inside scoop says the dog's walker has a lot on her mind these days.

She's a prosecutor hiding out at her sister's after suffering a brutal attack, and she's not out of danger yet. Thankfully, our Marine doesn't hold grudges, and has been seen doing a bit of reconnaissance over at Wags & Walks. Here's to hoping these two end up spending this **White Christmas** together.

❄ ❄ ❄

We've got quite a storm heading our way, but I have a feeling no one's going to mind being snowed in.

Stay safe and warm everyone, and Merry Christmas!

~Candy

Contents

I'll Be Home for Christmas

Ruth A. Casie

Beth Alexander, best-selling romance writer, has lost her muse, her fan base, and maybe the loyalty of her beloved agent. Sales of her new release plummet on the best seller list, and her contract with her publisher is in jeopardy. A heat-of-the-moment social media comment about a rival author goes viral, and not in a good way. No one knows that the rival author is the stuff male cover models are made of, least of all Beth Alexander. She heads home to Havenport, Rhode Island for a Christmas book signing, and a chance to lay low and let the storm pass.

Beth's chance encounter with a handsome, witty stranger has her heart racing, and her muse seemingly back. But, will the new story line she's created save her career? Or will her handsome savior betray her and turn out to be her worst nightmare?

❄ ❄ ❄

Dedicated to ~

The Scribes have become more than a group of authors writing short stories together. We are a team of compassionate, thoughtful, strong women who continue to learn and grow. I am so proud to be part of the team. Hugs to Emma, Lita, Nicole and Julie.

To our close friend DC Stone for her help at the eleventh hour to help us out. You are amazing in so many ways.

To Paul for supporting me on faith never having read a word.

I'll Be Home for Christmas
by Ruth A. Casie

SENT ADRIFT, a new novel by NY Times, USA Today best-selling author Beth Alexander should be just that, sent adrift! A heroine who is SOOO perfect is bor-ing. Jo Dee is a master chef, karate expert, and has an advanced degree in quantum mechanics. Next she'll perform a triple bypass on Detective Ryan's heart. Oh, that would mean he had one. OMG he's just plain stupid! He has as much depth as a puddle of water on a hot New York City sidewalk in the summer. Thank goodness for Jo's Irish Setter, Brandy. The dog has more personality then her hero. SPOILER ALERT. If you've read any of Ms. Alexander's last eight books just change the location and the villain's name and you've read this one. Then there's talk, talk, talk, gibberish, gibberish, no romance whatsoever, sounds like the author's life, doesn't it? Beth, darling, stop writing gibberish and TRYING TO PASS IT OFF as romance, call your writing what it is GIBBERISH!! Take a lesson from JD Watson's Jack Daniel series. Now there's an author who knows how to write.

"Ouch." Beth Alexander stood at the writing table in her favorite room at the Havenport Inn. She loved the dark green and white chintz with slick black furniture. It created a modern yet cozy atmosphere. But the warmth drained from the room. She read the review again. The words sliced through her with the precision of a surgeon's scalpel. Her hand trembled at her throat to protect what was left of her jugular. This wasn't her first bad review, and it wouldn't be the last. Strong feelings about a story and their characters were fair game, but this personal attack had little to do with her book.

"Only a small minded, unprofessional—" She couldn't think of enough adjectives. Who would assault her through her writing? She scanned the article and at the bottom of the page her offhanded attitude took a hundred-eighty degree turn. She gasped for air and released the paper. It fluttered to the table. She couldn't tear her gaze away from the reviewer's name. It was seared into her brain as if it were branded. Roberta.

Three months ago, Beth found herself on a live chat with JD Watson, and had attempted to be cute with the new romance writer who had made a big splash on all the lists. Maybe she had let the chat get out of hand. Everyone who knew her understood her sense of humor. Okay, so the banter came out more sarcastic and condescending. In retrospect, she could have kept the bitchy bits under control. But really, how often would she have the opportunity to chat with Watson? Still, the shit storm caught her off guard. Even JD rose to her defense, but couldn't defuse the situation. She stood by helpless as her fan base shrunk on all her social media networks.

But Roberta.

She wasn't a faceless fan. Roberta was flesh and blood. She was her friend.

Roberta's on-line newsletter, *The Romance Review*

Circle, with its wide circulation, became a mecca for romance readers who wanted to connect with authors. In three years the newsletter became the go-to publication for quality information on new books. Since Beth's first book, Roberta had become her most avid fan, and the brains behind Beth's Brood. The unique fan club supported her book signings and always arrived armed with a box of home baked cookies and her favorite treat, a bag of jelly beans.

A one-woman show, Roberta organized book themed parties for her new releases. And Beth took care of her. She made sure she sent swag and gifts. If she couldn't appear in person she'd call or web cast in, which always caused a flurry of excitement. Roberta helped name Beth's characters and suggested settings for her stories. Jeez, she picked out Brandy's breed.

She should've seen the shit storm coming. It started with Roberta's scathing public note calling her out for her attitude during the chat. Nothing she did would calm Roberta. She apologized. Even published a clarification on all her social media platforms, but the damage was done. The incident happened in September, almost three months ago. The uproar had quieted and her fans trickled back. Things had been rocky but now they were back to normal.

Evidently not.

Beth reread snippets of the review. An agonizing moment ticked past, and the reality of Roberta's opinion sunk in. She shuddered. Roberta had betrayed her—again.

Fisting her hand, she crumpled the review and threw it at the wastebasket. The ball of paper hit the rim and bounced onto the floor, no score, like her book. She let out a pained sigh. At least the review wouldn't impact her release-week sales stats.

Brush it off, move on. It's just one review. She pulled her computer out of her carry-on bag and started it up. It wouldn't take long to shoot off a response. The voice in her head, the one AWOL during the live chat, bellowed a loud, *no*. She glanced into the mirror and knocked her head with her knuckle. "Hello, anybody home in there? Go ahead. Dig yourself into a deeper hole." She let out a snort. Hole? Damn, bottomless pit described it better.

Her laptop whirred, chimed, and opened to her calendar. A reminder flashed. Jean Fedderman, her agent, would call today to let her know where she hit on this week's *New York Times* and *USA Today* lists. Her early books in the Jo Dee series made one of the top three spots on their respective launches, but since her ninth book in the series the launches had only reached number six. Her last book fell to number ten. She winced. It would be good to be back in one of the top three spots.

The second alarm chimed. Eric, her former roommate, had programmed the reminder before he left three years ago, right after she cemented her position as a top romance writer. She had her dream and Eric had his—to live among an uncivilized tribe in New Guinea. Really? She understood dreams, but Eric had his priorities; hot showers, Starbucks coffee, and five-star restaurants. The night he told her of his plan she practically fell off the bar stool. He never watched *National Geographic*, he didn't like adventure movies. Hell, he didn't like camping. But he sold what he wasn't taking, packed the rest, and left without a backward glance.

They weren't lovers. Oh no. She wanted to wash that picture out of her mind. They had a mutual respect. Best friends since college. He had encouraged her writing, critiqued her work, and his quirky sense of humor and timing was the inspiration behind Detective Ryan, the recurring hero in her series.

They tried to keep in touch, but with unreliable communication they promised to touch base every year before Christmas. She'd sent her note two weeks ago and eagerly waited for his.

The muffled sound of, "Your brother is trying to reach you on your cellular device," called from her handbag. She rummaged for her phone and swiped the display. "Hi, Brian."

"Beth, it's Linda. You get in all right? We've been glued to the weather channel all morning. There's snow all around the area."

"Yes, I'm safe and sound in Havenport. My luggage is another story. It's off on its own vacation—to Boston."

"You're so matter-of-fact about these things. I'd be ranting." Not completely true. Her sister-in-law knew how to deal with emergencies. A cardiologist's wife and a physics professor at MIT, her mathematical mind craved structure and organization. She made order out of chaos.

"I called to make sure you got our text. Brian had an emergency." Being late to family functions was par for the course. As the head of cardiology at Mass General, he rarely got to any event on time.

"I've checked with your brother and sister. Beau's running late refereeing a karate match, and Bernice is catering a private party tonight. None of us will get to Havenport until tomorrow. There's one key and we have it—"

"That's all right. I got your text. I'm checked into the Inn. When you speak to Bernice, make sure she brings the marshmallows. I can't wait for her cordon bleu s'mores."

Linda chuckled on the other end. Everyone teased Sissy, the family's pet name for Bernice, about her desserts. A fantastic pastry chef, she made delicious, elaborate treats. The family taste tested every new creation and awarded each with a s'mores rating. She never scored below four—the family's running joke.

"I've already put the fixings in the car." They both laughed and the sting from the review faded. "We're set to pick up Beau at his dojo and Sissy at her apartment on our way through Providence. We'll be there in time for the signing. It's been three years since we've all been together at the house. I can't wait."

"Me neither." Beth said her good-byes and ended the call.

So far this homecoming had its hiccups. She had imagined her luggage arriving with her, the family happily together, and her career back on track. She sucked in a deep breath. Mom said things happened in threes. She'd had hers. The rest of the holiday should be smooth sailing.

Once her mom and dad retired to Florida, she, her brothers, and sister decided to take over the family house in Havenport as their vacation get-away. Okay, she hadn't been back in three years, but not being able to join them didn't mean she didn't love it. After all, she set *Sent Adrift* in Havenport.

If there was ever a time she needed a safe haven, time to do some self-examination, it was now. For the last three years she navigated her course without a map or a rudder. She glanced at the balled-up paper on the floor. *It's one review. It's one bad review. It's one person's opinion.*

How did JD Watson capture everyone's attention? She knew exactly why those books were on the best seller's lists. She'd read the first three chapters of JD's last book and didn't have to read the rest. The story and characters were great. The hype, all of it, was well deserved. How could she hate a writer who could breathe such life into a hero, make him real? By the end of the third chapter she more than cared about the hero. She wanted to be the person next to him, fighting with him.

Her hero, Detective Ryan, had been strong and real, damaged, but able to come out stronger on the other side. Where was *that* Ryan? Could Roberta be right? Had her books become formulaic? Had she lost her muse? Would she ever find it again?

She picked up the crumpled review from the floor and put it into the wastebasket. Right now she needed to get through this book signing and delve into the research books she'd reserved at the library. She wanted to concentrate on home and family the rest of her vacation. Her career…well, she'd worry about her muse after the holidays.

One more glance in the mirror before she left. Every hair of her buster brown cut was in place. Turning her head from side to side the pained expression on her face startled her. A deep sigh left her parted lips. With a monumental effort she ironed out the frown from her wrinkled forehead to her down-turned mouth. She grabbed her makeup out of her bag and brushed on a dusting of blush to brighten her cheeks. She had her public image to uphold. Her clothes were travel weary but that couldn't be helped. Her trim five foot three inch body passed muster. A feigned smile in place, she grabbed her handbag, and left the room.

Outside she shivered from the cold frosty air and snuggled into her coat. The forecast had been upgraded from a possibility of snow tomorrow to get-the-snow-blower-ready-today, it's going to be a doozy. Shit, her practical snow boots were in her Boston-bound suitcase. She stared at her Jimmy Choo half boots and cringed. It took forever to find the right shoes for this outfit. She'd deliberated before she spent eight hundred and fifty dollars on the footwear, but she'd caved. The boots were perfect for the ensemble.

She headed down Main Street and passed stores

decked out for the holidays. Christmas lights twinkled in windows. Replicas of nineteenth century cast iron streetlights were decked out with wreaths and silver bells that chimed in the wind and wished everyone a Happy Holiday. The aroma of pine and cinnamon filled the air. One deep breath brought her back to memories of hot chocolate and whipped cream at the diner after holiday shopping with Mom. A breeze tugged at her and brought her to the present. She pulled her coat around her. The bookstore, The Final Chapter, wasn't far. If she hurried she could finish and be back at the Inn before the first flake fell.

She rushed down the four block obstacle course dodging patches of snow and ice until she stepped in front of The Final Chapter. Her ankle twisted and her other leg shot out from under her. The leather soles of her Jimmy Choos provided no traction. The man next to her dropped what he held and grabbed her before she fell.

"You all right?"

Startled, her head snapped in the direction of the rich deep male voice. She gazed into brilliant hazel eyes. Electricity skittered over her skin nestling in her girly parts. He stared at her as if he knew her—for a long time. Self-conscious, she pulled her gaze from his and concentrated on putting weight on her foot but winced. "Whoa," he said and held her tighter.

Her Hero wore a red and black plaid work shirt and washed out jeans. His broad shoulders and trim waist were romance cover worthy. His hands held her upper arms, and she wasn't in any hurry for him to let her go. Neither was he.

"Fine, thanks for the rescue," she lied. Heat rippled up her neck and hit her cheeks. She followed his gaze, which had traveled from her face to her feet and back again. He gave her a disapproving glare that melted her bones.

"Nice boots, but they won't work here."

She lifted her foot and examined her shoe.

"My practical ugly ones are in Boston with my renegade suitcase." She gazed at him through lowered lashes.

His face lit in a broad playful smile and caught her off guard. She never imagined a smile would warm her all the way to her toes, and other places.

"Think you can stand now?"

Must I? She planted her foot on dry pavement and attempted to stand on her own. "Thanks for your help. It's a bit sore but I can manage," It wasn't a total lie.

"You sure?" He loosened his grip, a warning he was letting go. It had been nice while it lasted.

There was a pensive shimmer in his eye as he removed his hands, but kept them close to her arms ready to catch her, again. For a split second she contemplated feigning a fall but deception wasn't her thing.

"I turned it. I'll be fine." She put some weight on it. "See. Thanks for coming to my rescue."

"It's not every day I get to play the hero." He glanced at her feet. "Good luck with your renegade luggage." He picked up the boxes. "We'll have to 'catch' up again." His eyes twinkled.

She couldn't control her burst of laughter. She was rewarded with a sexy smile and a torrid wink.

He reached for the bookstore door.

"Here, let me," she said, and held the door for him. He weaved through the racks of books. His back was broad and with the leather jacket he wore banded at his hips she got a full view of his butt, tight and cute. Military popped into her mind. He disappeared into a back room.

Ideas percolated in her head. She gazed across the

street at the Led Zeppoli—Italian Pastry Shop. A bookstore clerk by day, her hero could be a private eye by night, doing surveillance on a mafia ring that worked out of The Led Zeppoli. The pastry shop could be the front for a shake-down operation. No. She looked toward the bay. They could use the waterfront for drug smuggling. That's it, and Brandy, on vacation visiting family with Jo, sniffs them out and helps the hero close them down. She'd text the concept to her sister and brainstorm the story later.

Beth peered at the back of the bookstore where Her Hero had vanished. Still holding the door, she refocused on her objective, going over the book signing with Susan. She glanced at the poster in the window. Her press photo along with Winnie Boyle's smiled back at her. She looked forward to catching up with Winnie. They'd met on an author's panel at a conference and hit it off. They'd talked vacation spots. She mentioned Havenport. Winnie recommended the Celestial Harbor Resort on Star Island in the Virgin Islands. It was a great place to visit and write. She'd finished *Sent Adrift* sitting on the beach watching the boats sail by.

She stepped into the bookstore and was bombarded by images of JD Watson's and Winnie Boyle's books everywhere—the table in front by the door, posters at the ends of aisles, DVDs with audio versions on the rack next to the cash register. Over at the romance section *Sent Adrift* sat off to the side on an endcap. The endcap. It wouldn't have been so bad if the extra shelving unit was positioned at the end of an aisle but this endcap was off to the side and out of the main flow of the buying public. For the signing her books should have been all over the place along with JD Watson and Winnie Boyle.

Reveille trumpeted from her handbag and her flash of anger dampened. She pulled out her cell phone. "Hi, Jean."

"I got your text. You cracked me up with your suitcase on an excursion. Any news?" More than her agent, Jean also navigated the waters enabling Beth to do what she did best. Write.

"The airline said I'd get it tomorrow. I'm at the bookstore. My books aren't on a front table. I can almost make them out on the endcap in the far corner of the store." Silence. Jean was never quiet. The hairs on the back of Beth's neck stood in salute.

Wait a minute. She'd had three bad things already. She was home free. Wasn't she?

"You used to have me sign at top events, created events for me. You even took care of bookstore displays." Beth stood there and leafed through JD's new book.

"I'll speak to the store owner. I'm sure it's a slip up."

Beth's nerves calmed. She was seeing demons around every corner. Thank goodness for Jean. She could always talk her off the ledge.

"I bumped into the stock boy before. Maybe he hasn't gotten around to setting out my books. I'll work it out with him." She conjured him up without his plaid shirt and worn jeans, which wasn't hard to do, and the thought made her warm all over.

"I wanted to let you know about Roberta—"

"No need," she told Jean. "I already read her review. I'll let you know if I need a transfusion. I lost a lot of blood. She aimed for my jugular. The bandages will be off tomorrow before the book signing."

"Beth, you know I love your stories." Sure Jean did. The plate number on Jean's Lexus was Detective Ryan's badge number.

"There's more to a story than your heroine," Jean spoke with cool authority.

"What's wrong with Jo? She's smart, clever, self-sufficient, and able to think outside the box." Jean loved Jo, didn't she? The silence lengthened.

"Not Jo, Ryan. In his own way your hero has to be as strong as Jo." Beth's chest heaved and her temper flared. She knew exactly how she wanted Ryan to be. Her readers swooned over his defined abs and hulking muscles. They rooted for the unassuming blonde without any police training who gave Ryan the one clue that would break the case wide open and save the day.

"You agree with Roberta." Another betrayal. People turned and gaped. She boldly met their stare. If fire could come out of her eyes, the bookstore would be in ashes. Onlookers quickly glanced away. Her defenses were worn thin. Jean. She had counted on her agent. Was there anyone she could trust? Battle weary, she retreated to a distant corner of the store before she completely fell apart.

"Ever since Eric, your hero has lacked—"

"What has he lacked? He has all the vital parts." She lowered her voice and struggled to keep it as unemotional as a blank page.

"It's more than gratuitous sex scenes. Those don't move the story forward or show character growth."

"Eric, really? You know we didn't have any intimate relationship. For god's sake, the guy's gay."

"Think about it." Jean ignored her outburst. "Think about it is all I'm asking you to do. Let me go and call Susan about the setup. I'll speak to you tonight." The call ended.

"Think about it," Beth muttered. She'd tell Jean what she thought, bristling with indignation. What was there to think about? Erotica—the hot new thing. Perhaps she should take Jo in that direction. No, Jo was a private person. She wouldn't let anyone in her bedroom. She slipped her phone into her handbag and pushed thoughts of Jo aside for now.

She needed to straighten out the book situation here and see Wilma at the library. She glanced at the wall clock. Too early for the library. A movement caught her attention.

Her Hero navigated through the rack of books toward her. He carried his tall body with an air of self-confidence she found attractive. As soon as their eyes met a vague sensuous pull passed between them. Her heart pounded and her pulse ran wild. She met him halfway up the aisle not realizing she had moved.

"Hi, I'm Beth Alexander. My books and DVDs are on the endcap. They should be on one of the front tables, by the register, and every other place near the Watson and Boyle books especially for the book signing." He gave her a quizzical stare, then a Bruce Willis smirk broadened into a smile. She melted. Right there on the spot. Into a pool of soft, heated butter.

"I'll take care of your books and DVDs as soon as I'm done here, Ms. Alexander." His silky smooth voice had a playfulness that fascinated her.

"Thanks." She headed toward the racks and got lost among the romances. She chose a JD Watson book. She'd judged contests and analyzed characters. Were Watson's heroes in fact compelling? She found a place to sit and planned to skim the book. One more chapter she told herself after she finished chapter three, but quickly got lost in the story and the hero and had to read on. A few hours later she closed the book, sad she'd come to the end. She hadn't been wrong about the hero. He was deep, complex, and very male. For four hundred pages she had been with him every step of the way and now she couldn't ignore the emptiness without him.

After paying for the book, she stepped outside. A light dusting of snow blanketed the ground. The clock in Led Zeppoli's window said three-thirty. For a moment she debated not going to the library, but she had spent a lot of time on the phone with the librarian. Books had been reserved for her. Once this last piece of research was done, she could finish her edits and be free for the rest of the holiday. She headed toward the library.

Last week, her blog had included an excerpt from her work-in-progress. The scene had Ryan's gun, a Glock, drawn with the safety on. An anonymous person, obviously in law enforcement, mentioned she had it all wrong. Who knew a Glock didn't have a safety? To be accurate, she wanted to research the Glock and check on police procedures she mentioned in the story. The final manuscript was due to her publisher the week after Christmas.

She danced around the small patches of snow and ice, trying to save her shoes. The cold wasn't as brutal. A deep sniff—ozone. You never forgot that smell. As a kid it meant making snow angels and helping her brother build a snow fort.

She kept walking on until she realized her toes were wet. Her beautiful tan boots, aside from dark wet stains, were going to have horrible salt stains. More than the outrageous price she paid for the boots she had spent weeks hunting for the right shoe. These were the last pair in New York City. They were perfect. Shit, who was she kidding? Eight hundred and fifty dollars and she'd worn them three times. There was nothing she could do but hurry on. One more block and she'd be there.

She stepped inside the library, passed through the vestibule and into the reading room. Her old hangout hadn't changed. Comfy, overstuffed chairs were scattered strategically, filling corners and arranged in small conversational groupings.

With a deep breath, she reveled in the scent of paper, ink, and glue. She let it roll through her. Familiar. Home.

She headed to the research area on the right, searching for the librarian. She found Wilma putting cleaning supplies away. Beth's lips pulled in a smile. The woman had been there as long as she could remember and had always been a stickler for fingerprints on the glass exhibit case. Wilma's spray bottle was legendary among the high school set and stayed close at hand.

Beth gave herself a shake. Enough nostalgia. If she worked fast, she could find the information, edit her manuscript, and be done in thirty minutes. She caught Wilma at her desk.

"Hi." Wilma gave her a blank stare. "I called ahead and had two books reserved." Wilma knew who she was, she could tell by the recognition in the woman's eyes, but she didn't say a word. Strange. Beth had spoken to Wilma last week about what she needed. A large supporter of the library, she kept in touch with Wilma every month and sent books and swag to the Havenport Library along with a financial donation.

Roberta's news article sat prominently on the desk sending Beth's stomach into a deep dive. Wilma voiced her opinion loudly in the live chat. Now she understood why the woman ignored her. How many others would treat her the same way?

"I took them off the shelf and put them in the back room," was all Wilma said before she hurried away. While Beth waited, she brushed off her shoes and determined they were probably beyond repair. Was her career in the same predicament? A bubble of panic floated to the surface, but she burst it quickly. *One bad review. Get over it.*

"Here you are." Wilma handed over the books and returned to what she'd been doing. Beth was usually pretty thick skinned. Not today. Today her mood veered sharply toward anger. It took her a few minutes to realize she had to take a breath. Wilma's reaction had her between seething and sobbing and seething was winning out. *Deep breath. That's it. Focus on the research.*

She marched to the large conference table at the back of the room. Her shoes squished and left wet footprints on the carpet. She glanced over her shoulder and breathed a sigh of relief. Wilma hadn't noticed. Thankful, she continued on to the table, surprised to find Her Hero bent over a book.

She went to sit, but her oversized bag brushed against his books and knocked them to the carpeted floor with a muffled *thump*. As she reached for them, the ones she carried slipped out of her hands and fell on top of his books with a loud *bang*.

She bent down to retrieve her research books as he leaned over for his. Their faces close, she took a deep breath. Mixed in with the fragrance of books and ink the aroma of bay and cinnamon hit her senses.

He reached the books first, lifted his chin, then glanced at her. There was a spark of emotion in his eyes that made her heart stop. His lips were full and she was sure they would be soft to touch, to kiss. A flash of heat engulfed her centering in her girly parts. Someone let out a low moan. Her? Him!

"I'm sorry," she murmured and got up. Wilma gave her a dirty look and shushed her. She took the books he handed her and slid into a seat.

She needed to focus on anything but him. Her boots. They were a disaster. Rummaging in her bag, she fished out a tissue. Once she worked the snow packed boot clasp open the boots slipped off. They were in worse shape than she imagined. The meager tissue in her hand wasn't going to help.

"Here, let me." She glanced at Her Hero. He stood in front of her, his hand out, with an old newspaper, a rag and the spray bottle Wilma had used on the glass case.

"I beg your pardon." *Focus Beth*. He hadn't made a difficult request.

"Your shoes." He nodded at the stained boots. "The tissue won't help." He took them from her. "If you want to get the salt off the leather you need vinegar and water."

"How do you know the bottle has vinegar and water?" What a stupid question. One whiff and anyone would know.

"I wish I could tell you I deduced it from the smell, which would be a pretty good answer." He put the nozzle of the spray to his nose and jerked his face away. "But I watched the librarian fill the bottle with white vinegar and water." He stuffed her shoes with the newspaper then sprayed the solution onto the rag and rubbed out the stain.

Once he finished, he examined his work from every angle, then he pursed his lips and nodded. "Not bad if I do say so myself." He handed her shoes back. "Let them dry."

The vinegar and water solution was versatile. The white stains had vanished. She had recently read how a male lead used the same solution to get rid of the telltale water ring on a wood coffee table in a murder mystery. "Thank you. I don't even know your name."

"Jarred—"

"How can I repay you?" She put the boots down and dug in her handbag. He covered her hand with his.

She flinched at his strong, yet gentle touch. A shock raced through her and muddled her mind even more.

"No payment necessary." He drew his hand away, taking its warmth. Her brows wrinkled with disappointment. "I like helping damsels in distress." He threw out the rag, gave the cleaner back to Wilma, and returned.

"Guns and police procedures. Interesting reading. You don't look like law enforcement," he said as he took his seat.

"I'm not. Just checking some facts," she said, shrugging off the answer. Relieved he didn't dig deeper. His knowing grin suggested he knew about law enforcement.

"What are you studying?" she asked, leaning over expecting to see adventure, mystery, or science fiction. Instead she was startled to find psychology books.

"I'm researching the differences between men and women and the way they handle stress in relationships." He returned to reading his notes. His buff appearance had led her to think "athlete" rather than "scholar." Her cheeks heated at the realization she'd made an assumption based on his appearance. She knew better, especially since she was a woman's advocate. Outward appearance didn't make the woman, or the man.

"What have you found?" She pushed her research aside, more interested in what he had to say.

He put his pen down and sat back, his casual manner indicating he wasn't in any hurry. A glint of humor lit his eyes, and an easy smile played at the corners of his mouth. The thrill of his obvious interest in her buoyed her spirits. Her smile broadened, it was the polite thing to do, although polite never entered her mind.

"Men tend to be task-oriented, not at all talkative. They're more action oriented when it comes to dealing with emotions. Faced with a woman's emotions, rather than listen, they try to fix it."

That made her think. Visions of how her Detective Ryan reacted to Jo Dee ran through her mind. They weren't in line with Jarred's conclusion. Startled and intrigued by the revelation that Ryan's reactions were more like those of a woman.

"Women, on the other hand," she responded before he could say another word, "are intuitive, especially about the nonverbal cues like tone, emotion, and empathy.

Because they're good communicators they do well in groups, talk through the issues, and focus on how to create solutions that work for the group. You're right. When men are faced with a woman's emotion, they go right for the solution. But solutions are the last thing she wants. A woman wants comfort, cuddling, and empathy."

"Interesting." He chuckled. "Men are not known for their empathy." He brought his chair closer to hers. "Like stress," he said. "Under stress, men exhibit the "fight or flight" response."

Beth nodded. She hadn't considered the differences in gender reactions in that context. "Women don't think fight or flight, at least not initially. Under stress they work to protect the group. It has to do with protecting the young and seeing to the family unit. They also think very differently about sex."

A sly smile brightened his face. She wanted to slam her hand over her mouth.

"They do?" He dropped his voice to a low raspy whisper and sent chills, the good kind, up her back and to other places.

"For a woman, sex starts in their head, not necessarily between her legs." Shit. Her face was so hot she was going to go up in flames. Jeez, that's what Jo Dee would say, definitely not Beth Alexander.

"Oh really?" If she thought his soft, male mellow voice or his smoldering stare couldn't get any sexier, she got that totally wrong.

"I'm a romance writer. I write about relationships and emotions," she replied.

"And sex," he added. Was he extending an invitation? She wasn't a loose woman, but she was more than tempted to say yes. And that was her notion, not Jo Dee's.

Dangerous territory. He needed a diversion as far away from the topic as possible. Battleships. He filled his mind with great big ships cutting through water, anything that didn't include Beth Alexander and sex in the same breath.

"Why do you write?" he asked her. It was a simple question, but he knew there wouldn't be a simple answer.

"I have characters in my head. They pester me to tell their story. I can't ignore them and," she added in a wistful voice, "I can't not write."

He knew that drive. "What's the hardest part for you?" He wanted her to keep talking. He'd read all her books and studied everything about her. Did she have any idea how rich and sensuous she made her stories? They bombarded him on every sensory level. As a reader he wanted to protect her heroine from every bad encounter and nasty event. Beth's stories were filled with heart and compassion. How the hell did she do it? Why couldn't he?

Her brow wrinkled as she stared over his head. She wasn't going to give him a quick canned answer. No, instead she gave the question a lot of thought. Tilting her head to the side she gazed at him. He was taken back with a glimpse of the real Beth Alexander. This woman was strong, witty, and open. The rolling battleship on the rough seas morphed into a sail boat in calm waters.

God, she was beautiful. He stared into her smoky brown eyes. He wanted to make them smolder. The cut of her hair framed a heart-shaped face. He stared at her lips and pondered how soft and luscious they would taste. Her body was perfect, curved in all the right places.

"You work for months to get the first draft. Then you edit and rewrite. In the end you're proud of your work and launch your new baby. It's a happy time." She paused and was pensive. "You may be lucky. Your readers love it. But if you lose sight of the prize, the writing, you lose a piece of yourself. That's the time you become vulnerable." She shook her head but her eyes watered.

Shit, she must've read Roberta's review. He'd call Roberta and have her make this right. What was he thinking? Beth told him women don't want a solution. They want to be comforted, held. Dare he?

Before he could decide, she glanced back at him and the openness was gone. She opened her book. Maybe he got it wrong. He took the hint, left her alone, and returned to his books. Every so often, he raised his gaze and stared at her. This was more than a fan moment. Now what?

His cell phone vibrated. He had a text message. It was Marc MacDonald, an old Marine buddy who owned the auto shop in town. His brakes had acted up on the drive into town. He hoped Mac could take care of them.

Got the part. Car ready tomorrow. Need a place to stay? I've got plenty of room.

He sent Mac a quick reply thanking him for the offer but he had a room at the Inn. The car taken care of, he glanced at Beth who was reading about handguns. He wasn't surprised by her research topic but he had to hold back his smile. *No Beth, Glocks don't have a safety.* He settled into his seat and picked up his research where he had left off.

"Excuse me," the librarian announced. "Please finish up. The library closes in fifteen minutes."

Six o'clock. Research was a singular process for him. The solitude good for concentration, but isolating. These past few hours sitting across from Beth were comfortable and productive. He'd filled up pages in his notebook. He glanced at her. She pulled the newspaper out of her shoes.

"Here, let me help you with that." He took the shoes out of her hand. Kneeling in front of her he grasped the heel of her foot. The intimate touch had him breathing hard. It made her giggle.

His face turned up, one eyebrow raised.

"I haven't played Princess of the castle since I was a kid and my brother got too old to play the Prince. We'd use Mom's clear plastic high heels for glass slippers." She let out another giggle, which got her a loud *shush* from Wilma.

She had no idea how her unassuming joy and the intimate touch affected him. He slipped the boot on her. "Ah, m'lady you must be the Princess." He stood and gave his best attempt at a courtly bow before he formally offered her his hand and helped her to her feet.

She stood up and gave him a kiss on the cheek. Her neck flushed and when he gazed into her eyes intelligence and friendship stared back at him. That was something to build on.

The moment passed and she broke away, gathered her things, and stepped over to Wilma's desk to check out the armful of books she'd accumulated. Finished with Wilma, she headed to the door.

He packed his things and returned his books to the cart. Out of the corner of his eye he admired the sway of her hips and shape of her leg. She was dynamite in those high heel boots but in this weather she'd kill herself. He straightened his shoulders and stepped up beside her at the library door, ready to leave.

He followed her gaze out the glass door. There had to be six inches of snow on the ground.

"I have to get to the Inn," she murmured. The rumbling of a motor and loud scraping sound caught his attention. Through the falling snow, yellow lights flashed and the snowplow came into view. The lumbering truck pushed the snow aside, clearing the street down to the asphalt. It moved slowly past the library.

"If we follow behind the plow you might be able to save your shoes," he said.

"Or else we'll have to come back and borrow Wilma's spray." He smiled at the trace of laughter in her voice.

He opened the door for her. The air smelled frosty and cold, but close to her the scent of vanilla and spice captured his attention. He helped her off the curb.

No way would she be able to navigate the slick surface wearing those boots with all she carried. He slung her computer bag over his shoulder and took half of her research materials.

A tentative step and she slid on the slippery street. He put his free arm around her and tucked her into his side for safekeeping. "Ready?" he asked her. She nodded and they followed the snowplow, creating a small parade.

"I was thinking about what you mentioned earlier regarding a woman's sexuality. Men think differently than women," she said. "A woman's sexual turn-on is more complicated than a man's." He fumbled with the books he held. Her words froze in his brain.

"You mean women don't think about sex as…enthusiastically as men?" This wasn't new to him. Every guy knew women weren't instantly turned on. But he'd never philosophized about or discussed sex. Not with a woman.

Beth's voice dropped to an intimate whisper. With her tucked close to his side, her fragrance, and talking sexual attraction had him breathing hard. He wanted to take her in his arms and find out how soft and delicious her lips tasted.

"Oh, women are enthusiastic but we need… a plot, like a novel," she blurted.

The idea clicked in his mind. "Ah, romance, a build-up—"

"Yes. It's the anticipation, even for a casual encounter."

Now it made sense. Clinically speaking, the build-up gives a woman time to receive and interpret the message on an intellectual level, then send the signal to her body parts for arousal.

"I understand. A woman has to connect with a man to have sex, while for a man, sex is the connection." She stopped and gazed at him with those big brown eyes. He wondered if his signal was getting through to her. His heart pounded against his chest loud enough for her to hear. A wind swept down the street and she shivered.

"Jeez, you're cold." He pulled her closer and moved them on.

They entered the Inn. The blast of heat from the fireplace defrosted him as he stamped the snow off his shoes. She did the same. He stared at her boots.

"They seem fine," she said. He escorted her upstairs, still carrying her computer bag and books.

"I had a great afternoon. You don't have to walk me to my room," she said as they climbed the stairs. He gazed at her flushed face, not sure if it was pink from the cold or the closeness they established.

As she opened her door, he pulled the computer off his shoulder and placed it inside. Before he could say a word, she put her lips on his. They were soft and inviting. Better than he anticipated. He deepened the kiss not knowing where this would lead and not caring until the sound of feet tramping up the stairs reached his ears. They broke apart.

"I better go. Thanks." She slipped inside. The latch closed with a *click*.

He stood there staring at the door before he trudged down the hall to his room.

Shrugging out of his parka, he took his notes out of the oversized pocket and hung his coat on the back of the door. He threw the notes into his open attaché case on top of his new Jack Daniel manuscript then grabbed a towel to dry his hair.

The fragrance of vanilla and spice, soft brown eyes and a passionate kiss— Beth Alexander was etched in his mind. He didn't want to spoil the connection they had made, but if he didn't tell her he was JD Watson, it was destined to fail. Maybe it was doomed before it began.

He tossed the towel back into the bathroom and paced the small space. "Hi Beth. I think you should know I'm JD Watson." *Shit.* He stopped and faced the dresser mirror. "Beth," he said and pushed his hand out toward the mirror. "I never introduced myself. I'm Jarred, JD Watson." *Fuck.* He wheeled around and slammed his hand into the bathroom doorjamb.

At first he thought it funny she mistook him for the stock boy. Why didn't he tell her his name at the library, or on the way here? He paced more. *Be direct.* He stopped at the mirror again. "Look Beth, I'm JD Watson." He shoved out his hand.

Gathering his courage, he left his room and headed to the bar for a peace offering.

"How can I help you Mr. Watson?" the bartender asked.

"A bottle of Riesling and a couple of glasses, please. Charge it to my room." In Beth's bio she mentioned she enjoyed Riesling. While he was filled with courage he took the stairs two at a time and knocked on her door.

"It's open," she yelled, her voice coming clearly over the open transom window above the door. He entered. She stood at the small desk, her back to him. "Put the fax on the coffee table, please."

He had moved from stock boy to hotel bellhop and

wasn't sure if it was a promotion or a demotion. He coughed, loudly.

She turned and her face lit in surprise. His courage shriveled along with his male body parts.

"There's someone at the door. Speak to you later." She ended her call and came over to him. He handed her the bottle and put the glasses down. Bad move. Once he told her his name, she may want to hit him over the head with it. At least his hands would be free to protect himself.

"I'm sorry. I assumed you were the bellman with my fax." She examined the bottle, then gave him a sheepish smile. "I enjoy Riesling. Thanks." She put the bottle next to the glasses. "I'm glad you're here. I wanted to apologize for kissing you. It was spontaneous and…"

He crowded her space and her voice trailed off. He raised her chin with the crook of his finger and stared into her eyes. There it was. The connection. He cupped her head and brought his face close to hers. Passion filled her eyes. It drove him on. He dipped his head and kissed her. She remained still. He deepened the kiss, and she opened her lips. Then he took her in his arms—

A tap on the door broke them apart with a gasp. "Your fax, Ms. Alexander." She stepped out of his arms and opened the door. The bartender must be doing double duty. He stood there with the fax in his hand. Jarred panicked the moment the bartender's eyes lit with recognition. The last thing he wanted was the bartender to call him by name. Jarred put his finger to his lips and hoped the man got his signal. The bartender gave him a knowing smile.

"The front desk said you needed this right away." Beth dug into her pocket and gave him a tip. He left, but she didn't close the door. Jarred flexed his hand itching to shut it and pick up where they had left off. He glanced at her face. The softness was there but the passion was gone. The moment had passed.

"Have dinner with me." He gave her his best smile with every intention of convincing her to say yes, but she stepped to the other side of the coffee table, putting a barrier between them. He didn't want to believe all was lost.

"Thank you, but not tonight." She paused, then continued in a sinking tone. "I'm on deadline and need to finish this manuscript by tomorrow. Please understand."

"Sure," he said. He struggled to keep his smile from fading, then stepped out into the hall.

She rushed around the coffee table. Her hands grasped the door frame. "Stop by the book signing tomorrow and we can talk more."

He put on a brave face. "I'll be there."

He headed to the bar. He ordered a hamburger and a tall beer. What was he to do now? Coward wasn't a word he wore willingly, but it fit. He finished his hamburger and drained his beer as his cell phone rang.

"Hi Jarred. You set for the signing tomorrow?" If anyone would understand his predicament, it would be his agent, Jean Fedderman. Always a font of information, she was full of ideas.

"I bumped into Beth Alexander at the bookstore this afternoon." Silence.

"No scene. She thinks I'm the stock boy." Jean burst out laughing. "It's not funny. She has no idea who I am. We spent the afternoon together." That made Jean stop.

"Jarred, for months we've discussed how your stories lack the feminine view. You've called Beth a true artist, maybe this is an opportunity to get her woman's point of view. It wouldn't hurt to give your stories a feminine touch."

Jean had a point, which didn't solve his current

problem. "You haven't told her JD Watson will be at the signing."

"Didn't I? How neglectful of me." A flash of anger exploded at her sarcasm but he kept himself in check. His fist quietly pounded the table. Maybe it was time to troll for a new agent. Jean was great, but he didn't like playing games, especially with a person's feelings involved.

"The two of you need to talk for lots of reasons." If Jean only knew. "Both of you are awesome writers, but can help each other. You're not competing. There's room for you both. Please, talk to her. She may be smarting from Roberta's article, which will be nothing as soon as she hears she's dropping on the lists, but I know you two can help each other."

"Are you crazy? Now is not the time, especially after Roberta's review. Don't you have any feelings?" Another beer magically appeared. He nodded his thanks to the server.

"But—"

"But nothing. You listen to me. Beth and I should have been informed of everyone scheduled to be at this event. Not telling us was a bad idea, a really bad idea. I don't like your tactics and I don't appreciate the position you've put me in." Was he being fair? This fiasco was as much his fault as Jean's.

He heard her house line ring. "I have to go," she said. "It's Beth's publisher. I have to call Susan at the bookstore to check on your poster. When I spoke to her yesterday, she hadn't received it. I'll call you as soon as I'm done." The call ended.

He rubbed the back of his neck then took a gulp of beer to cool off. What a hell of a mess. He couldn't let Beth walk into the signing without knowing he was JD Watson. He glanced at the stairs, chugged the rest of the beer, and signed the tab.

Whatever spark they'd ignited would be doused, drowned out, and he could do nothing but stand by and watch. He racked his brain but found no way to prevent it. He climbed the stairs like a condemned man to his execution and stood at Beth's door, his hand poised to knock.

"Hi Jean, I have you on speaker phone. I had time and researched the Glock issue. I have to give it to the anonymous blogger. Glocks don't have a safety. I found some other issues that need editing. I'm almost done with the rewrite. I've strengthened Jo and I think it's time to retire our Brandy, make him a hospital therapy dog."

"Leave the dog. You have a whole following of Irish Setter lovers. You don't want to jeopardize losing them. Instead of making Jo stronger, maybe you should give her a weakness."

"No, I don't want to make Jo vulnerable. People want to read about strong heroines, not damsels in distress."

His hand was still ready to knock. He empathized with what Jean told her. It wasn't long ago Jean had strong-armed him and helped him whip Jack Daniel into shape. It wasn't easy to hear, but Jean hadn't steered him wrong. The desperation in Beth's voice made him ache. She fought hard to save Jo, Ryan, and Brandy. He wanted to kill Jean for the way she handled this. He raised his hand higher.

"Any news about the lists?" He hesitated. Jean was quiet. "I didn't make the top three. Okay, where did the book place in the top ten?" More dead air.

Oh, Beth. He stood by helpless.

"It's not all bad," Jean said. "It's sitting solidly at twenty-four."

"What do you mean it's sitting solidly at twenty-four?" A chair scraped against the wood floor. Her voice high and shrill. "What the hell is that supposed to mean?" He lowered his hand. He knew her next question.

"Where's Watson on the list?" Silence. Beth wasn't going to like this answer.

"Three of Watson's books are on the list and are sitting at first, second, and ninth spots." She sniffled. He leaned his forehead on the door. No one spoke for some time.

"I've given this a lot of consideration. Now it's crystal clear. Do you think my career has peaked? Am I a descending star?" Her voice was a whisper.

No, Beth. Her star had blinked, not gone out. He wanted to crash through the door, take her in his arms, and make it better.

"I'm sure it's the residual effects of the shit storm over the live chat. It will die down and your numbers will rebound. You know how fickle fans can be."

"Sure, I know. I also know it takes one incident for people to desert you, move on to the next author, and never come back."

"I want you to speak to JD—"

"Jean, please, don't tell me about JD Watson. Yeah, yeah I know. JD's the next best thing since sliced bread. We both know that author's a flash in the pan whose star will burn out quickly."

He knew that wasn't true. He'd watched her reading his book at the bookstore. Genuine emotions ran across her face. She was into the book one hundred percent. Besides, he'd worked hard to avoid being a "one hit wonder," and succeeded. There were ten Jack Daniel stories. Yet, it had to suck for a talented, amazing author like Beth to feel the aftereffects of being pushed off her peak. Either she was deep down a bitch—which he didn't believe for a moment, his instincts weren't shot yet, or she hid her hurt, trying to deflect. Perhaps he did understand the female psyche more than Jean would admit.

"Speak to Watson, that's all I ask. I think you two can help each other."

"How can you suggest that? Speak to Watson. About what?" A loud slap on the table made him flinch. "I wonder what Watson's agent had to do to get those books on the list. Besides, I found a new hero, the bookstore stock boy. I had this idea—"

He walked away from her door not wanting to hear anymore. *Maybe things will be better in the morning. Yeah, sure.*

Beth woke to someone knocking on her door and attempted to focus on the digital clock on the bed-stand. By the third knock, the time came into focus. Nine-thirty. "One minute," she croaked.

Without her luggage, she slept au natural. Thank goodness for the fluffy white robe the Inn provided. She shrugged into it and padded to the door.

"Good morning, Ms. Alexander. It's nine-thirty. I have your breakfast." She opened the door and the bellman rolled in a table. "The temperature is 25 degrees and it's snowing." He handed her the morning paper. She gave him a tip and her thanks. "Enjoy your day," the bellman said before he left.

She went back to bed and stared at the ceiling. It had been a fitful night; tossing and turning. One minute her career was over. The next minute she jumped out of bed to jot down notes about her new story idea. Even Her Hero made his way into her dreams. The warmth and sincerity of his kiss was... worth investigating. Flirting was fun, but they had connected on a deeper level. She looked forward to seeing him at the book signing. He sounded positive when she asked him to stop by. At least there was one bright spot.

The aroma of the hot coffee called to her. The taste of buttery toast would help make up for the horrible night's sleep. Time to face the day. Business first. She checked email... The fragrance of cinnamon toast wafted across the desk reminding her of Her Hero and left her smiling.

Her computer screen came to life. How could she have this much junk mail in one day? She prioritized the most important and dumped the rest. Halfway through the inbox she spotted a message from Roberta. She had some nerve. She saved that message for last.

There was a message from the airlines—subject: Missing Baggage.

Dear Ms. Alexander –Your suitcase is due to arrive from Boston late this afternoon. As soon as it arrives we will deliver it to the address you provided. We apologize for any inconvenience and thank you for flying Air Rhode Island.

Looked like she was going to wear yesterday's clothes.

She read and dealt with the rest of the messages. After twenty minutes, Roberta's email was the last one left. Her subject line, *I'm Sorry*, intrigued her.

Beth, after much thought and discussion with a trusted author, I realize my review was malicious and unprofessional. All of the women in Beth's Brood stand behind you. I had planned to come to your book signing today and apologize in person but the weather here is bad. We have two feet of snow and it's still falling. I've removed the post and will put up a new review before the day is over. You have every right to be angry with me. Friends don't do that to each other. Ever.

She sat back and reread the message. A small sigh escaped her lips. She was glad Roberta recanted her words but the harm was already done. People would remember the personal attack and scorching review, not the retraction. But there was a degree of satisfaction in Roberta's intent. She sent a simple reply, *All is forgiven,* before she closed her computer and peered outside.

Snow. The piles of plowed snow in front of the Inn would make it sloppy going from here to the bookstore. Susan, the bookstore owner, had been excited about doing the signing the week Beth's story released, and had contacted her publicist to work on promotions. Hmm, she should contact her publicist and see what she could do with Roberta's new review, but that would have to wait.

She stared at the bottle of Riesling on the table and smiled at the lingering decadent thoughts she had about Her Hero. She couldn't count the number of ways she'd undressed him in her musing. He never disappointed her.

The more she thought about him replacing Ryan in a new series, the more she knew she was on the right track. She sat down and had a fit of writing. The words flowed. She stopped to pick at her breakfast and pour more coffee. By eleven-thirty, she had a detailed outline and two character studies.

With the book signing at one o'clock, she had to get herself in gear. She showered then attacked her hair with the small pick in her purse. Her clothes were another story. Where was a fairy godmother when you needed one, or your luggage? She glanced at her rumpled travel clothes: wide leg slacks, long silk oxford shirt, an oversized sweater with a wide bottom band, and a black blazer.

Thank goodness she had worn tights under her slacks. She grabbed the freshly washed tights she hung in the bathroom last night. A quick glance in the closet and she located the ironing board and iron. She ironed the long silk shirt then scrutinized her travel sweater. The soft mohair sweater had been on many flights with her and had seen better days. A few clips with her nail scissors and she removed the wide bottom band. Next she examined her pants. A white ring of salt stained both pant legs. They'd never do. She pulled off the belt. Everything lay on the bed.

A few minutes later she stood in front of the long mirror studying her new ensemble. Black tights peeked out from underneath her long freshly ironed crème colored blouse that reached her knees. The first two buttons open, she pulled at the collar and tilted her head. She opened another button and smiled. She cinched the blouse at her waist with the dark tan belt. It wasn't ideal. She wished she had the silver link belt in her luggage.

Moving on, she slipped on her black blazer and pushed up the sleeves. The broad waistband of her red mohair sweater turned into an infinity scarf that she wore loosely draped across her shoulders. The red made the outfit pop. Not bad.

She put on her shoes. "You poor things. I don't think you'll survive this trip." Her coat on and bag in hand, she opened the door and stopped in her tracks. A pair of bright red galoshes perched on top of a box sat in front of her door with a note tucked inside one boot.

Anything to save the Choos.

She laughed at the pun and crushed the paper to her chest, tearing up at his thoughtfulness. She couldn't wait to kiss him.

She exchanged her Choos for her new red boots. They fit like a glove. How would he know? Of course, when he cleaned her boots at the library he must have noticed her size. She ran down the stairs and made her way through the lobby and outside. She reached the street and rushed on ready to test her new red galoshes in any convenient puddle of slush but Havenport had done an excellent job of clearing the roads. She checked her watch as she turned the corner. It was twelve-thirty. Perfect, the bookstore waited up ahead.

People jammed into The Final Chapter. She peeked in the window. Her books were on a front table. Maybe she'd give Her Hero two kisses. She headed around to the back and entered by the staff door.

"Beth, I'm glad you made it." Susan gave her a large hug. "Sorry I couldn't speak to you yesterday." She led Beth to the pegs to hang coats.

"That's all right, your stock boy was a big help." Susan gave her a strange look. "But—"

"Susan, sorry to interrupt. Hi, Ms. Alexander." Marcie, Susan's cashier, nodded from the door. Beth waved back. "We need you up front."

"Go," Beth shooed Susan away. "I've done this hundreds of times."

"Thanks. We'll speak later." Susan and Marcie rushed out the door.

Beth peeked in the back room, eager to see if Her Hero was there but the room was empty. Maybe today was his day off. She let out a sigh, picked up the bags of promotional gifts, and headed for the signing table. On her way, she scanned the room and checked out every man until she was dizzy from wrenching her head back and forth. She was acting like a sixteen year old and loved it.

Winnie Boyle dropped everything and bolted out of her chair when Beth entered.

"Hi Winnie. How was your trip in? Biscotti. What a wonderful surprise." She gave Winnie a hug and took one of the homemade cookies on Winnie's table, eager to take the first bite. The crunch, the chocolate, and the nutty sweet taste were perfect with coffee. Even Bernice would be impressed.

"I should have come by sleigh. Thanks for

contributing your new book to my treasure hunt. We had great participation," Winnie said.

"No problem. I had a good time with the fans. I hope it helped sales." Susan gave her the high sign. "It's almost one o'clock. Let me get my stuff set up. We can talk later."

Beth sat in her seat at the other side of the table. Her cloth and runner positioned, she found her books in a box under the table and set them out. Cover cards, bookmarks, and her trademark bowl of jelly beans were set and ready.

She reached in her handbag for her favorite signing pen and noticed the blinking message light on her phone. There were two messages. One, a text from Linda. Brian was still at the hospital and they wouldn't be leaving for a few more hours. Linda was sorry they would miss the book signing but would see her at the house. She sent them an 'OK.'

The other message was a voice message from Jean. Jeez, four minutes—long for a voice message. That one would have to wait until later. There was an empty seat between her and Winnie and she wondered whose it was. Before she could steal a glance at the books beneath the table, someone slipped into the seat next to her. Her Hero.

"Hi. I'm glad you could make it." She bent close to him so no one else could hear. "But you can't sit here."

His face twisted in a pained expression. She was immediately concerned. He pulled books out from under the table and stacked them in front of him along with bookmarks. She stared in horror as she read the cover. JD Watson. He kept his head down as he busily arranged the space. Books, bookmarks, even his cell phone lay on the table between them. He never looked at her.

In the back of her brain she recalled his name, Jarred,

he had said. Her heart fell to her feet, then slammed into her throat.

He caught her gaze, leaned over and put his hand on hers. She pulled it away as if burned by a brand. He sat back. The muscles on his face were hard as glass.

She didn't speak. She didn't trust herself to say anything; afraid she would shatter into a million pieces.

"I tried to tell you last night." His tone was even and controlled.

"Before you kissed me," she snapped. She attempted to hide her pain and anger, but her throat tightened and she had trouble swallowing around the hot knot growing there.

"That's not fair, Beth. We both wanted that kiss."

Her mouth flapped like a beached fish until she found her voice. "And you played along. Did you enjoy the joke, you and your agent?" She blinked quickly. *Don't you cry in front of him.* She struggled to keep her chin from quivering.

"What I said or did came from my heart. It wasn't a game. I. Don't. Play. Games," he said through clenched teeth.

How absurd. He was angry, as if he had any right to be. She wanted to be any place but next to him. But she was trapped here for the next three hours. Perhaps if she got rid of her books she could go to the house and wait outside for the others.

Susan opened the event and introduced each author. Thank God she called Winnie first. Beth struggled to pay attention, but Jarred's profile kept drawing her back. The strong line of his jaw. The curve of his lips. The shadow of his beard.

Winnie read the back cover copy of her new book and a cute anecdote about time travel.

Susan introduced JD Watson and announced his new

book had been picked for a movie option. The crowd, already excited, erupted in a roar. Any remaining JD Watson books were grabbed off the tables and shelves. It took several minutes to get the crowd quiet.

Unbelievable. His cheeks were flushed and his head down. Modest. Embarrassed. *Bullshit.* It was all an act. Beth sat looking straight into the crowd, a Mona Lisa smile on her lips.

"Mr. Watson," a reader called out. "Who do you think will play the lead roles?"

"Hush," various people said in the crowd trying to get everyone quiet.

"There's talk of some 'A' list stars teaming up, but I've been sworn to secrecy," he said sending the crowd into another uproar. Beth tried not to glance at him but she did. He was shining like a bright star. She remembered that feeling. It made her loss worse.

She scanned the area searching for her quickest way out. This was the last place she wanted to be. Every second was an eternity. The tension between her and Jarred built. About to jump out of her skin, she needed to escape. She was half standing. His strong hand grabbed hers under the table and held her in place. She made an effort to pull away but he held her tight. With a smile pasted on her face she sat down and tuned everyone out. It was the only way to get through listening to the fawning and accolades.

Susan called her name and introduced her as Havenport's own. He took his hand away. She held her breath afraid no one would care. The crowd exploded louder than they had for Jarred. He stood pulling her up with him. He returned to his seat and applauded the loudest.

"Thank you," she said over and over nodding trying to make eye contact with as many people as she could.

"Thank you."

No one had any idea how grateful she was or how humbled by their outpouring of affection. After a deep breath she picked up her book and read the back cover copy. Everyone listened carefully, pockets of excitement exploded around the room as she identified a store, street, or a favorite hangout. Finally finished, she sat and the signing began.

Jarred's cell phone rang. She had a conditioned response to cell phones, she glanced at the display. She wasn't being nosey but she knew that number. She considered it for a few seconds before realization hit her. "Jean," she blurted. She stared at the phone then Jarred in disbelief.

He answered his phone.

Jean. Her chest squeezed tight. Jean was his agent. She blinked quickly to stop tears that threatened to come down her cheeks. She sat there numb.

"It's for you." He handed her his phone. "She's been calling you all morning."

She took his phone and put it to her ear but didn't say a word.

"Beth," he coaxed gently.

"Beth, you there?" Jean said. She closed her eyes. What a fool she'd been about Jarred, Jean, Roberta, even writing. "Listen, I'm sorry to do this to you, but I've called and texted you all morning. I know you're there until the late afternoon but MacMillan is threatening to cancel your Jo Dee contract. I pitched a high level concept of the story you told me about last night. They're interested. They like the concept and the genre change. We have a great opportunity for a long series possibly even a TV option. They want to know more. I need more detail so we can close the deal."

"Not now, Jean." She didn't recognize her own

voice. *Betrayed* flashed in her mind like a neon sign. By Roberta, by Jean, and by Jarred. "We have a lot to talk about, the least of which is my contract. I don't want to talk to you now." Jared put his hand on hers. She flinched and looked at him in shock. He hesitated but pulled his hand away before she slapped it. She turned her back toward him.

"I'm going to finish this event, then spend the weekend with my family. Tell MacMillan the earliest I can have a concept to them is Wednesday." That should satisfy Jean and get her off the phone.

"Beth, it's business. Jarred needed an agent and I was searching for new talent. I made him an offer."

"Yes, I'm well aware it's business. Sharpen your pencil Jean because after the holiday I'll be in the market for a new agent. You'll have plenty of time to find new talent." Someone moaned. Jarred. She wasn't surprised he'd been listening. She closed her eyes and breathed hard. *Steady. Ignore him.*

"It doesn't have to be this way. I've always had your best interest in mind the same way I do for my other authors. Think before you do something you'll be sorry for later."

"I don't have to wait for later. I'm sorry for a lot of things." She ended the call and left his phone on the table without looking at him.

With a smile plastered on her face, she greeted fans, answered questions, and signed books. Inside she was numb on one level but the little voice in her head kept talking to her. Ninety minutes later, the authors took a break.

She disappeared out the back door. The cold air slapped her in the face. She leaned against the cold brick wall, her head back, eyes closed. Sleet bombarded her face like tiny pin pricks. She wrapped her arms around herself and sniffled. Her sniffles turned into tears and quickly gave way to sobs. Slowly, her back scraped against the rough bricks and she sank to the ground. She buried her head in her knees and cried.

Strong arms picked her up and pulled her close. The warmth was comforting. She knew the scent of him. It was Jarred and, God forgive her, she didn't want to be anywhere else. He stroked her hair, held her until her sobs subsided.

"Feel any better?" he asked. She nodded, unable to speak. He reached into his pocket, pulled out a handkerchief, and put it in her hand. She wiped her eyes and blew her nose. Why did he have to be JD Watson? Why couldn't he have been a stock boy?

"We've got to get inside. Will you be all right?"

She gazed into his eyes. They were warm, but she hesitated. She couldn't go through this pain again.

"Good. We'll talk as soon as we're done here," he said. He kept his arm around her and they went back inside.

The signing over, everything was cleaned and packed. Marcie led Winnie, her sister-in-law Jane, Jarred, and Beth out to the back parking lot while Susan locked up the front.

"The forecast is for deep snow with white out conditions. I'm glad you don't have far to go," Marcie said.

Everyone agreed. Beth gave Winnie and Jane a hug. They had already agreed to meet up later in the week to 'talk shop.' Jarred and Beth watched them traipse out.

She picked up her bag without a word and headed toward Main Street. Tears streamed down her face. She was an emotional mess on so many levels.

He touched her shoulder sending shivers down her spine. She closed her eyes, thankful he'd stopped her. "You're not going anywhere." His voice was deep and rough with concern. "Not now." She turned and faced him. She knew those firm sensual lips and she wanted them on hers. She sucked in her breath when her gaze reached his eyes. They were filled with passion and tenderness. She stood with him in the parking lot not speaking just staring into each other's eyes.

Headlights flashed into the parking lot. She squinted to see who it was. A Range Rover with a snowplow fixed to the bumper stopped in front of them.

"Thanks for bringing the Rover, Mac. Need a ride back?" Jarred asked.

"No, I'm not going far. See you." Mac left without another word.

"Your chariot, Princess." Jarred opened the passenger door. She glanced at him quizzically. "Mac is an old Marine buddy. I had him put a plow on my Rover. Come on, get in. I'll take you back to the Inn."

"Thanks, but I'm not going to the Inn. My family finally got here. I'm going home."

"I'll drive you." An agonizing moment slipped by as his stare held hers.

JD Watson had been her Moriarty, her bigger than life nemesis, but he hadn't used her. If anything, she had used him as her scapegoat, the reason for her failure rather than face the truth.

Finally, he voiced with gentle sincerity, "Please."

She could use that little voice right now. AWOL, again? Coward. She didn't wait to hear it, and instead got in and closed the door as he put her things in the back.

"Where to?" He waited with his finger poised over the GPS ready to type the address.

"It's five miles outside town. No need for the GPS."

She motioned to the dashboard. "I'll navigate. Make a right when you get to the street."

"You need to know I had no intention of deceiving you." He brought the Rover to the end of the lot and made the turn.

"But—"

"No, let me finish. It's been twisting my insides for the last two days. Jean arranged for me to do the book signing. For me, it was a great opportunity to reconnect with Mac. I didn't realize you'd be signing too until I read your blog and your Tweets. I called Jean to make sure you knew I would be here. She told me she doubted you knew she represented me. She promised she would tell you in plenty of time. I thought you were teasing when you treated me like a stock boy. As soon as I realized you had no idea—"

"I believed JD was a woman." She had to laugh thinking about it. No wonder he wrote great heroes. He understood the man's perspective; he was a man. All man. Remembering his touch, his kiss, her scalp tingled and her breathing faltered. How stupid she'd been.

"That was intentional. Jean and my publisher didn't think women would read a romance written by a man. As soon as I realized you had no idea who I was, I wanted to use the time for you to get to know me, the real me. And after we kissed…" He was quiet for a long time. "Do you truthfully think you would have given us a chance if you knew I was JD Watson?" he asked quietly.

"No. I may be objective, but not where JD Watson is concerned." This could have been handled much better if Jean had been up front. All right, her agent had asked her to speak to him, but Jean shouldn't have tricked her. Stock boy. That was funny. Their conversation at the library wasn't. It was sincere and they connected. She couldn't be wrong. It wasn't what they spoke about, but how they listened to each other. And there were the little things. Thoughtful things. She turned in her seat to face him.

"You asked me if I would have given our connection a chance if I knew you were JD Watson. No is the simple answer. But now I know who you are and I want to give us a chance."

He stopped the Rover. "I know what I want. You. But I'll give you time for your head to connect to your other body parts." There was his drop-dead smile again with his smoky passionate eyes.

"And are yours already connected?" With a slight shake of her head she laughed.

"Yes, ma'am." He drove on. "In all the right places."

She needed to change the topic. "I'm thinking of starting a new romantic suspense series but I need help with my hero. Your hero, Jack Daniel, is so real. There are subtleties in how he moves, how he thinks. I can't capture it on paper." It wasn't a bogus question. She wanted to understand how he wrote.

"I have the same problem, but for my heroines. I was researching women's reactions when we met at the library. You're the star of capturing the driving force of character with the emotional vulnerability that makes Jo Dee believable. I can't write like that."

"Together we have the hero-heroine problem covered. We should collaborate…" The idea fell out of her mouth and startled her into silence.

"Are you serious?" The *swoosh* of the wiper blades and the muffled rumble of the motor filled the cab. "It's not a bad idea. Actually, I'm intrigued. I'd be willing. How about you?"

"It could be a fun project." Jo Dee and Detective Ryan had run their course. It was time for new beginnings in several areas of her life. She gazed at his profile and the voice in her head agreed. "I have to give my publisher a completed concept for a new series by Wednesday. We can speak to Jean." She glanced out the windshield. "It's the next right."

He pulled up to her family's house. As soon as they got out, Sissy threw open the door. "Hurry up. You're letting in the cold. Your suitcase arrived about thirty minutes ago along with a package from Eric." They rushed in, stamped the snow off their feet, and stowed their coats.

"Cute boots," Sissy said. She bent to Beth's ear. "Who's tall, dark and handsome? And did you bring one for me?" She kissed Beth's cheek then turned to Jarred.

"Jarred, this is my sister Bernice, Sissy for short." Jarred shook Sissy's hand.

"You're a brave man coming to meet us all at once." Sissy took them into the large family room. Frank Sinatra's "Mistletoe and Holly," a family favorite, played in the background. The rest of the family stood around the end table devouring the appetizers.

"You two better get started before the hordes pick the plate clean." The oven timer rang. "Dinner will be another twenty minutes." Sissy hurried around the other side of the kitchen island where Linda attended to the pots on the stove.

"Jarred, the two with the stuffed mouths are my brothers, Brian and Beau. That's Brian's wife, Linda, at the stove." With their hands and mouths full, the brothers nodded their hello.

"Linda? How'd she get in the family without a 'B' name?" he murmured to Beth.

"Her real name is Belinda," she whispered. He chuckled and shook his head.

"Yeah, it's funny," she said. "Secretly, friends whose names begin with 'B' always had an edge over the others."

"Really? I'm Jarred David Watson, Junior. My family calls me Bud to avoid confusion."

"I wish I had known that earlier." She laughed. "Everyone, this is Jarred Watson, Bud for short."

Sissy stopped plating dinner. "Watson? Any relation to JD Watson?"

"That would be me," Jarred said.

"Welcome. Let's get your plate filled, but don't get too full. Sissy brought four desserts for taste testing." Brian led Jarred over to the buffet. "Sorry we couldn't get to the signing. How'd it go?" He handed Jarred a plate, then popped a stuffed mushroom in his mouth.

Beth went into the kitchen to help Sissy and Linda.

"Jarred and I are thinking of collaborating on a romantic suspense series." The men brought in empty plates. "I'll have to come up with a strategy. Changing genres can be tricky. I don't want to upset my fans. They expect a romantic comedy with Jo Dee and Ryan. I may have to change my name."

"Use your real name," Beau said, picking at the melted marshmallows on the sweet potato soufflé. Linda swatted his hand away.

"Beth isn't your real name?" Jarred asked, finishing his spinach dip and crackers. Beth almost snorted her bruschetta. "Not Beth. Alexander is my pen name."

"I agree with Beau. Use your real name." Sissy offered spooning the juices over the rib roast.

"Ten more minutes until dinner," Sissy announced.

"Let's see. The tag line could be—The desire of romance with the thrill of suspense by Holmes and Watson." She turned to Jarred. His eyes widened in surprise. "What do you think?"

"Elementary," he said. The others hooted and laughed. She held out her hand. Beth took Jarred into the glass-enclosed porch. She stood with him and stared at the falling snow creating swirls of sparkling light around the outside lamps. Strains of Frank Sinatra's "I'll Be Home for Christmas" filtered into the room.

"Come Holmes, the game is afoot," he said, taking poetic license with Holmes' signature line. He took her into his arms and they sealed the deal with a kiss.

About the Author

RUTH A. CASIE is *USA Today* Best Selling author of swashbuckling action-adventure, some are time-travel, all her stories are romances about strong empowered women and the men who deserve them, endearing flaws and all. Her Druid Knight novels have finaled in the NJRW Golden Leaf contest. The Guardian's Witch, part of the Stelton Legacy series was a Reader's Crown Finalist. Ruth also writes contemporary romance with enough action to keep you turning pages. She lives in New Jersey with her husband, three empty bedrooms and a growing number of incomplete counted cross-stitch projects. Before she found her voice, she was a speech therapist (pun intended), client liaison for a corrugated manufacturer, and international bank vice president in product and marketing management, but her favorite job is the one she's doing now—writing romance.

❄ ❄ ❄

Ruth loves to hear from readers, too, so drop her a line at Ruth@RuthACasie.com or visit her on Facebook: facebook.com/RuthACasie. She's also on Twitter: @RuthACasie. If you'd like to receive her newsletter and receive a free book, please sign up at www.RuthACasie.com. Thanks!

Winter Wonderland

Lita Harris

❄ ❄ ❄

Olivia Baxter struggles with her indecision to return to college and heads to Havenport, Rhode Island to visit her aunt during winter break. Memories of prior Christmas' emerge, and a chance meeting with an interesting stranger makes Olivia think twice about staying in New England or returning to her studies.

Max Porter has been searching for his biological parents, which leads him to Havenport, Rhode Island. He wanders into the Final Chapter bookstore and befriends Olivia, an open minded, and warm person who wants to help him find the answers to his past.

Together, the young couple discover new things about themselves that lead them to think about where their lives may lead next. Will they move on to the next chapter together, or go their separate ways?

Dedicated to ~

The readers, because of you, our stories can be told.

Ruth, Emma, Nicole, Julie, and Desi—you ladies rock and appreciate chocolate as much as I do.

Winter Wonderland
by Lita Harris

Snow brushed her nose. Olivia Baxter stood across the street from The Final Chapter bookstore. She smiled as her Aunt Susan hung an ornament on the Christmas tree in the storefront window. It had been a few years since she'd seen her late grandmother's best friend. Aunt Susan and Uncle Matthew made it a point to stop and visit during their trip to Florida each year, but Olivia had been away at school for their last visit. She'd been to Havenport a few summers when she was younger but never in December. *Brrr.* It was cold. Not at all like at home in Florida.

Havenport could be the perfect place to sort through her dilemma. Its small town charm, cobblestone streets, and benches along Main Street were inviting. Comfortable.

She hadn't told her mother she didn't plan on returning to college. She'd just completed the first semester of her second year and wasn't feeling it. Maybe she wasn't meant for college. The lectures were boring and she hated being holed up in a classroom most of the day.

She waited for the cars to pass, then crossed the street and approached the store. She clutched the front of her jacket to ward off the wind from the ocean. Her other hand hesitated on the doorknob. Maybe she should've called her aunt instead of showing up unannounced.

An overhead bell rang as she opened the door.

"Hello, Aunt Susan." She looked around the shop. "I know you're here. I saw you through the window."

Flames danced in the fireplace at the back of the store and promised warmth. She sat at the small table a few feet away from the flickering flames. She loved how the dry heat warmed her to the core of her bones. Not like that electric heat with its cold air pockets back home. She wiggled out of her coat and scarf, leaving her beret on because she thought it looked cool.

She remembered the old house in New Jersey with its seven fireplaces that were never used. Mom didn't trust the old brick chimneys and was petrified of a fire breaking out in the nineteenth century home. It was hard to take care of the old house, especially when her father left them for his "barely older than a teenager" wife and their new baby.

Olivia hated that day. Her mother in tears at the kitchen table. Her older sister Brianna didn't care. It wasn't long before Mom sold the house and packed them up to move to Florida, which Olivia never fully embraced. She preferred the change of seasons. Plus, she liked visiting her Aunt Susan.

She swung her legs over the side of the overstuffed wingback chair and stretched her back across the other side with her head hanging down from the soft as a pillow arm. "Aunt Susan. You've got a visitor. And she's hungry."

The food car on the train hadn't had much to offer. She didn't trust the tuna fish, and the fourth bag of potato chips left her stomach feeling blah. Or, maybe it was nerves and the inevitable discussion with Mom about not wanting to return to school in the spring. A few days with Aunt Susan would help her prepare for when her mother arrived. Her aunt had a knack for letting her know if she was wrong without making her feel terrible or stupid.

"Aunt Susan. I have something for you."

The cellar door creaked open.

"What are you doing here?" Aunt Susan ran over and hugged Olivia so tight her face buried in her aunt's ample breast.

"I—I..." She wiggled her head away from the overzealous hug. "Now I can breathe." She laughed.

"You surprised me." Aunt Susan smiled and brushed Olivia's hair away from her eyes.

"That's the point. I knew if I told you, you'd be stocking up your refrigerator for months."

Aunt Susan and Uncle Matthew never had children of their own and made Olivia feel like she was a daughter to them. She thought it was cute the way her grandmother, Emily, and Aunt Susan had married brothers. She missed her grandparents, especially this time of the year. The last day she'd spent with her grandmother was when they made cookies. She'd been ten years old and her grandmother died before they could eat the goodies for Christmas. The holiday hadn't been the same but her visit to Aunt Susan was sure to bring happiness this year.

She reached into her purse and retrieved an old box, pulled an ornament from it, and held it up to the light.

"Do you remember this?" She twirled it by the ribbon it hung from.

Aunt Susan clasped her hands to her chest.

"Oh my. Of course I remember that. Your grandmother loved it. Your grandfather made it for her soon after they met. He was a skilled craftsman." Aunt Susan cupped the ornament and smiled.

"I'm going to hang this on your tree." Olivia walked over to the front window and set the ornament with care. Ice skaters came to life as flames flickered from the fireplace and shadows bounced off snowflakes and mirrored skating rink inside the globe.

She'd never known of two people more in love than her grandparents. It was the one relationship that gave her hope when her own parents divorced. Life with Mom hadn't been pleasant after her father left them but Olivia wasn't about to give up on love.

"It hasn't aged at all."

"Grandma kept good care of it and I've kept it packed away until now. I'd look at it every Christmas but never took it out of the box."

Her aunt smiled and her eyes sparkled.

"You really loved her, didn't you?"

"Yes, I did. You never knew two people more opposite than us. Yet it was our differences that made our friendship what it was."

"Tell me." Olivia settled into the chair near the fireplace.

Aunt Susan spun the open sign to closed, and locked the front door. She pulled a chair close and lovingly squeezed Olivia's knee.

"Oh, where to start? It was my first day in a new school. Your grandmother was forced to make me feel welcome and show me around to my classes. All I wanted to do was find the cute boys. That was our first difference. Your grandmother couldn't care less about that. She was always a good student. She just wanted to study and get ready for college. I just wanted to have fun."

"Didn't she ever have fun?"

"Eventually." She laughed. "I was from a broken home, she wasn't. Your great-grandmother was really sweet to me and the next thing I knew, I was spending more time at your grandmother's house than my own. Anyway, I spotted Michael one day and thought I was in love."

"My grandfather?" She sat up eager to hear about the grandfather she barely remembered. She only had her grandmother's stories to hang onto and she missed those moments. She bit her lip to hold back tears—she missed her grandmother so much.

She curled up on the chair and waited for her aunt to tell her story.

"Yes." Aunt Susan lowered her head. "But it was your grandmother who stole his heart. Almost from the get-go. We went ice-skating so I could run into Michael but he literally ran into your grandmother."

"Grandma told me about that when I found the ornament." Olivia remembered that cookie baking day when her grandmother told her how she'd met the love of her life. It was the most romantic story she'd ever heard.

Would she find her true love?

So far high school and college hadn't been very promising in that area.

"So, skipping through that, um, she was the best friend I could have. Once she saw through my boy crazy ways and I saw how sincere she was we just clicked. I loved her like a sister and that's the simplest way to sum it up."

Olivia yawned and stretched her arms over her head. "I wonder if I'll ever have a love like my grandparents."

Susan leaned over and gently rested her hand on Olivia's knee.

"You will one day, dear. I'm going up to bed. The guest room is ready for you. Now I know why I was propelled to clean it this morning."

❄ ❄ ❄

Olivia was the first one downstairs the next morning. She sat on the window bench in the bookstore and watched the snowflakes fall in fits and starts. It's not like she wasn't used to snow, the years she lived in New Jersey had given her an appreciation for the white fluffy stuff. It gave her a sense of comfort. All was quiet and clean. Like a fresh start. College wasn't giving her the satisfaction she'd hoped it would. It didn't feel any different than high school had. She was empty inside. Something was missing from her life but she couldn't put her finger on it.

Heavy footsteps came from the staircase that led to the apartment upstairs.

"Good morning, Sunshine."

"Uncle Matthew!" She leapt from the bench and ran to him, hugging him tight.

"That's a nice greeting. I've missed you, too."

"I didn't even know you were here. Last I knew you were in Florida." She released her hold on him to let him catch his breath.

Aunt Susan followed behind.

"I got in late last night. You must have been asleep. Did Aunt Susan tell you the latest news?"

She turned to her aunt who lowered her head.

"No, dear, I haven't told her yet." Aunt Susan plugged in the coffee pot and put out a plate of brownies.

"Why? What's up?" Olivia narrowed her eyes.

Aunt Susan folded her arms across her chest. "I was going to tell you over dinner tonight but he can't keep his mouth shut."

"Is it serious? Is everything okay?" Her voice softened.

Uncle Matthew stepped back and moved Aunt Susan toward Olivia.

"Yes, we're fine. A bit tired of the New England winters and we've decided to move to Florida. That's all." Aunt Susan rested her hand on her niece's shoulder.

"For good?" Olivia's stomach sank. Havenport was her home away from home. It wouldn't be the same without her aunt.

Aunt Susan nodded. "For good. But you're old enough to travel on your own now, so you can visit anytime. We'll have a spare room."

Somehow that didn't make Olivia warm and fuzzy. She could count on her aunt and uncle to be there for her. Here. In their bookstore that she loved. A place that was familiar and made her feel welcome.

"What will you do with the bookstore?"

Aunt Susan hesitated. "We did have it up for sale, but no takers. There doesn't seem to be much demand for a business like ours anymore. The big stores have seriously cut into our livelihood."

Olivia did notice no customers came in last night but maybe it was an off night. *But they can't close the store.*

Uncle Matthew draped his arm around her shoulders. "We'd like to see the store continue. It was good for me when I retired my medical practice. Nice customers. Aunt Susan made this a special place but demand has changed.

Plus, we're old and I'm tired of shoveling snow."

She understood. In her mind they were the same people she'd met as a child. She hadn't paid attention to how they aged over the years.

"But until we leave, we'll be open. I have two author signings set up for this week." Aunt Susan unlocked the door and flipped the sign to open.

"How long will you be here?" Uncle Matthew asked.

"At least a week. Longer if I can."

"You can stay as long as you want. I'll be out most of the day. I have a few things to tie up. See you at dinner?"

"Of course, Uncle Matthew."

"Good. See you later." He kissed Aunt Susan on the lips and headed out.

Olivia waited until he walked out the door. "You're so cute together. What can I help you with today?"

"You came just in time. My staff is down. No sense in hiring someone when they won't have a job for long."

"I knew I was compelled to come here for a reason other than to visit you."

The doorbell rang. She nearly snapped her neck as she did a double take. *He's gorgeous!* She clamped her jaw closed to keep from looking like a fool. She watched him with a subtle side stare. His soft wavy hair enhanced his muscular profile. She figured he stood at least six-foot-one.

"You can start with helping Max. He just moved here. I met him yesterday at the corner diner."

Aunt Susan nudged her with her elbow. "Go ahead. He seems like a nice guy."

She froze—unsure what to do next. She'd never worked a day in her life and was fortunate that way. Even though her father abandoned her emotionally, he made up for it in substantial financial support.

"Seriously?" she whispered.

"Go." This time Aunt Susan nearly pushed her over the chair.

She smoothed her hair back and straightened her sweater around her hips and walked over to him as he perused the neat bookshelves. He tipped a book toward him with the tip of his finger and pushed it back.

"Good morning. Can I help you?"

He turned to her and her breath stilled. She'd never seen piercing green eyes on a guy. It was like he looked right through her. His little bit of facial scruff appealed to her. He was grittier than the college boys she barely endured.

She bit her lip. *Why am I nervous?* She crossed her arms to steady herself.

"What are you looking for?" She tried her best to come across as professional.

"A book about this region." He walked away from her.

She tried to follow him, but her legs trembled and her feet froze in place. *Pull it together girl.* She quietly cleared her throat and willed her body to move.

"The regional section is over here." She pointed to a bookcase near the door. She knew her aunt was watching her. "Anything in particular you're looking for?"

"No."

A man of few words. "Well, this is the shelf you want. I'll leave you alone. Ask if you have any questions." She walked over to the counter.

Aunt Susan came up behind her. "Cute one, isn't he?"

"He's gorgeous but doesn't talk much," she whispered.

"That so?" Aunt Susan handed Olivia a sign promoting the author event. "Would you put this in the window please?"

She took the sign and walked back to where the stranger mulled over the book selection. She took care positioning the sign so people saw it clearly from the street.

"This is my niece, Olivia, she's here for a visit," Aunt Susan yelled across the store.

Olivia wanted to die. She wished the floor would open up and swallow her. She settled for hiding behind the Christmas tree that stood between her and Max. She was sure the tree was shaking as hard as she was. How could her aunt embarrass her like that?

She couldn't see his face and hoped he couldn't see her. *One...two...three. Breathe.*

"What brings you here?" Aunt Susan interrogated him. "There's not much call for tourism here in December."

Olivia peered from behind the tree. She cleared her throat and stepped toward Max. It was better to come out of hiding than have her aunt continue to embarrass her.

"I apologize for my aunt. She likes to talk— especially to strangers." She turned to her aunt and motioned with her eyes to knock it off.

"I don't mind. I come from a small town where it takes an hour to fill up your truck with gas because no one can say hello and move on. I'm used to it."

He stepped away from the bookcase. "I'll take these."

He handed two books to Olivia.

"Marine life and seashells?"

"Yep."

"Whatever." She shrugged, and brought the books to the register for her aunt to ring up.

"You won't find much in the way of seashells on the beach this time of year," Aunt Susan said.

"Maybe not." He pulled out his wallet and handed over a twenty.

"Olivia can show you around. She's not doing anything." Aunt Susan put the books in a bag and handed them to Max.

"But, I'm helping..." She gave up. It was like the last time her aunt tried to fix her up with Larry the lifeguard during a summer visit. She sucked at small talk. It had been painful—he wouldn't shut up. But she knew her aunt wouldn't leave her alone unless she gave in.

Aunt Susan took a twenty out of the register drawer. "Go get yourselves some coffee down the street."

She rolled her eyes and took the money.

"Olivia. That's a pretty name." He took the bag from Aunt Susan and flashed a smile Olivia couldn't say no to. "I'd like that cup of coffee."

Her stomach flipped. Coffee wasn't going to sit well with her but she wanted to be nice to her aunt. And maybe Max would turn out to be an okay guy.

She put on her coat. "Follow me. You're in for the tour of your life."

※ ※ ※

The smell of coffee guided them to Corky's Cafe on the Havenport Marina. Men in business suits and others in fish gut covered jeans and T-shirts packed the place. Olivia stood for a moment to take in the diversity of the customers clamoring for a morning cup of energy. She let people in front of her since she wasn't in a hurry and everyone else seemed like they were. She backed into Max as she stepped aside.

"Oops, sorry. I didn't mean to squish you." She looked back at him with a slight smile. She tried her best to not bump into him again but the cluster of patrons knocked her about like a buoy in the ocean.

"Crowded in here." He looked over her head.

If she was going to spend time with this guy—she knew exactly what her aunt was up to—he needed to do more than look good. That alone wasn't enough to impress her. She'd spent enough time dating pretty boys. Even though they were never anything serious, she'd had her share of lousy relationships. She wanted something more than a cute guy who looked good next to her. She was going to get Max to open up with more than his observations of the weather and local population.

She turned to him. "Where are you from?"

"Pennsylvania." He nudged her closer to the counter.

"Where in Pennsylvania?"

"You've never heard of it." The corner of his mouth curled as if suppressing a smirk.

They were next in line. Her neck stiffened with annoyance. She turned around to face him head on. "How would you know what I know or don't know?"

He gently ushered her to the counter when the customer before them left. "Two coffees, regular, cream."

He'd said it faster than she could open her mouth. *Arrogant.* She reached into her pocket but, he threw a ten-dollar bill on the counter before she got out her cash.

"I can get my own..."

"Will that coffee work for you?" He took his change leaving two dollars on the counter.

She grabbed her coffee and took advantage of an empty table by the door. He followed her and took a seat.

"How did you know how I wanted my coffee or even if I drank coffee?" She leaned back and held the steaming cup with two hands up to her face.

"Was I wrong?" He sipped his coffee quietly. She liked that. Nothing worse than a guy slurping his drink.

She narrowed one eye and pursed her lips behind the cup. "No. Still, that's kind of arrogant, don't you think?"

"Wouldn't you have corrected me?" He cracked a faint smile.

He had a point. She would've corrected him. But, his assumption was still annoying, yet she couldn't steal her eyes away from his. Maybe that's how he'd become so bold. One good hard stare and a girl would accept whatever he told her.

But not this girl.

"Maybe. Apparently, I'm not as good at this guessing game as you, so again I ask. Where are you from?"

He stretched his arms wide over his head and looked slightly annoyed.

She didn't care. She needed to know who she was heading out to the deserted beach with in the middle of winter.

He took a drink before speaking and rubbed his eyebrow. "Mountwood."

"Mountwood, Pennsylvania?"

"Yes. Why? Are you going to make fun of the name?"

"No. Why would I?" She shrugged.

"Okay, nothing. Most people do that's all."

He sat back, finished his coffee, and twirled the empty cup on the table, staring down at it like he willed it to do something.

She sipped hers, not really liking the strong brew. She was used to the weak stuff Mom made. The thought of her mother coming in a few days made her cringe. She never knew what to expect. If she was in a good mood— things were wonderful. A bad mood almost guaranteed a miserable time for all.

She was going to have to have the talk. First, she would need to make up her mind. She sank into herself and took in the serenity of the sounds from the ocean. Maybe she could go back to Florida with her aunt and uncle, then she could walk on the beach year-round.

The lack of conversation with Max unnerved her. She had to get things started. "I don't see why. It's the name of your town, so what?"

He crushed his cup and tossed it in the trashcan next to them. "Most do that's all."

His rim shot wasn't lost on her. "Impressive. Play basketball much?"

"Nope."

She was getting frustrated but didn't know what else to talk about or how to get him to say more than three words at a time. She was going to get back at her aunt for making her his personal tour guide.

"How about we take a walk down to the beach?" She stood and hiked her handbag onto her shoulder. The door opened and slammed into her. Not the best place for a table. If she didn't get out of there soon, she'd turn black and blue.

"You don't have to do this." He got up and held the door open for her.

"You're right, I don't but I'm just as curious as you."

She plunged her hands into her coat pockets and watched him walk toward the water with his jacket wide open like the ocean breeze didn't faze him.

The weathered ramp had seen better days but it was sturdy enough to take them down to the sand. The wind wasn't as wicked as she expected it to be. Seagulls picked through remnants of the outgoing tide.

She stood back while Max walked up to the surf. It was too cold to take off—

"Wait. What are you doing? You crazy? Taking off your boots in the winter just to dip your toes in the ocean?"

She ran down to him, grabbed the back of his collar, and yanked him away from the water.

"What the hell..." He spun, dropped his boot, and laughed. "You're not an adventurous type, are you?"

"Are you nuts? It's freakin' December. Do you know how cold that water is? I'm not going to be responsible for pulling your drowned ass out of that freezing water if you fall down."

A rogue wave crashed into Max.

"I knew that was going to happen." She tried her best to stifle a laugh.

"Thanks." He straightened himself and stood with his bare foot planted in the cold sand and reached down for his seawater filled boot.

She stepped back in disbelief that he would head into the water in the middle of winter.

"Do you people always overreact like this? I wasn't going swimming. I wanted to feel the sand and water between my toes. That's all." He walked away from the coastline. "Sock's gone."

She squeezed her hands tight and backed away. "I'm sorry. I didn't want you to get knocked down. The undertow can be rough."

Time to head back. She was done with her good deed for the day.

"I can take care of myself." He walked past her with one soaked boot on his foot and the other in his hand. "I always have."

The cold didn't seem to faze him. He stormed away.

❄ ❄ ❄

Olivia walked back to the bookstore alone. She hadn't noticed what direction Max took when he left her at the beach. She suppressed a chuckle. It was mean to laugh at him but kind of funny watching him walking with a bare foot in the cold weather. Then she wondered what he meant as he left her. *I always have.*

"Hello, dear. How did it go?" Aunt Susan must have been baking. The store smelled of fresh brownies.

"It was interesting." She hung her coat on the rack and straightened the poster in the window. She wasn't sure what to make of Max, but he was as intriguing as he was irritating. She knew she tapped into something personal but wasn't going to push it. She'd already spoken to him more than she intended.

"Did you two have fun?" Aunt Susan sat at the goodie table.

Olivia joined her.

"There wasn't much to do or talk about. Anyway, there is something I need to discuss with you." She mustered up her courage and leaned forward. "I don't want to go back to school."

There it was, out in the open. It felt good to tell someone else what she'd been harboring for months.

Aunt Susan's jaw dropped. "You can't do that."

"Why not?" This wasn't the reaction she expected. Aunt Susan was the rebel in the family. The one who traveled to places no one heard of. Did things against the rules. Was open to anything new.

Various colored crystals hung from the ceiling. She couldn't identify them except for the clear quartz. They added something new to the bookstore and she liked them. Not typical of someone her aunt's age—proof she was different.

"You need to finish, and then go off and do what you want. Get your education taken care of while your father is still paying for it. I've always regretted not finishing my degree."

"Wow. That's not what I expected to hear from you."

Aunt Susan stood. "It was the one thing I wish I would have done differently."

"But why? You've had a fantastic life. Travel. I mean when you went to Africa when Uncle Matthew volunteered his time there. That was amazing."

Aunt Susan leaned down and hugged Olivia. "It was, dear. But I was there because Uncle Matthew was. The only thing I've done for myself is this bookstore and it's no more than a hobby right now."

With that, Aunt Susan strolled over to the one customer browsing in the corner.

Olivia grabbed a brownie and leaned back in the chair. If Aunt Susan, who was open to any decision, had regrets about not having gone to school, then so could she.

The bookstore had gone through some changes since the last time she was there. Small toys displayed where books used to be. There weren't as many tables of books as there were the last time she visited.

She sat back and watched her aunt talking with a customer. She couldn't make out what they were saying but smiles were exchanged so she knew it was her aunt's typical pleasant chit-chat. Olivia skin itched hanging around the bookstore. She needed to do something to work off her nervous energy.

The bookcase needed dusting so she picked up the worn-down-to-a-nub feather duster and wiped away at the books. She worked her way closer to the register and pulled out a book about shells. She flipped through the pages, intrigued at the large array of shells that were supposed to be on the beach but she'd never seen them.

What, were there people who got up before the sun who picked up all the shells?

She thought back to Max and pictured him as she'd seen him a few hours earlier. Crazy that he wanted to dip his feet in the freezing Atlantic. But that was her opinion, which didn't seem to matter much to him. Strange bird he was, and that got her curiosity kicked into overdrive.

Aunt Susan made her way back to Olivia.

"Back to what we were talking about. You have to stay in school. Period."

Olivia returned the book to its assigned slot. "I honestly don't know what I'm going to do. Maybe it's the school or my degree program. Whatever it is, I know I'm not happy."

She relaxed as Aunt Susan rubbed her shoulder.

"Well, that's something else. You haven't found your passion yet. Common problem with kids who start college right out of high school. Take some time off with the intention of going back."

"That's what I was thinking." Olivia could always count on her aunt to help her think through a complex situation. Just like when her grandmother died. Aunt Susan had helped Olivia work through her grief.

"Have you discussed this with your mom?"

She threw her head back and laughed. "Absolutely not. That is the one thing women in our family do. They go to college before anything else."

Aunt Susan smiled. "I know that well. That's all your grandmother focused on. I never would have gone if it wasn't for her. She always knew better than I did. I miss her terribly."

"So do I." The stale air closed in around her. She needed to get outside. Too much time inside made her antsy.

Plus, she might run into Max. She wanted to learn

more about him, no matter how difficult he made it. He seemed to be an okay guy—but his lack of communication skills sucked and it drove her crazy. That was reason enough to spend more time with him. His secretiveness sent her curiosity into overdrive.

"Aunt Susan, I'm heading out for a bit. Do you need anything?"

"No," her aunt yelled from the storeroom.

Snow again! Sheesh, it seemed like every time she stepped outside, a snowflake fell. She zipped her jacket. The salt from the sea hung heavy in the air. She loved being this close to the ocean, the smell, and the waves.

It would be getting dark soon so she headed toward the water first. She stood at the railing of the ramp and her body swayed to the motion of the water and made her at ease with the world.

The smell of snow in the air and saltwater was drizzled with the smorgasbord of aromas from Corky's.

She couldn't resist and was pleased that the deli was nowhere near as crowded as it was a few hours ago.

"A cup of hot chocolate, please."

"Anything with it?" the craggy man asked.

"Hmm, marshmallows."

"Whipped cream, too?"

"No, just marshmallows." She laid her money on the counter and waved away the change.

She left Corky's with hot chocolate in hand and walked down the ramp. The sun followed her as she got closer to the sand. The idea to stand barefoot in the surf tempted but she wasn't as brave as Max had been. She scanned the shoreline in search of him. She'd no reason to believe he'd be there. That still didn't stop her from hoping.

He wasn't anywhere in sight. She wandered along the sand slightly above the water line, high enough so her sneakers didn't get wet.

She spotted a man in the distance and stopped to make him out. *Not him.* It'd be easy enough to find out where Max stayed, but that might seem creepy if he found out she looked for him.

Oh, shoot! Mom was due to arrive in Havenport tomorrow. She finished her hot chocolate and headed back to the bookstore.

She'd have to make a decision about school before Mom arrived. This would be the last night of peace she'd have and she was going to take advantage of it.

A few flakes of snow landed on her nose. Her tongue stuck out to capture the pristine crystals as she did with her sister when they were younger. She missed the flakes and her sister and headed back to the bookstore.

"Did you have fun?" Aunt Susan was cashing out the register for the day.

"I did. It's nice on the beach this time of year. I didn't think it would be but it was."

Aunt Susan zipped the bank bag and put on her coat. "Uncle Matthew and I are going out for dinner. Would you like to join us?"

Olivia watched the sun fill the sky with a bright orange hue that bounced off the storefront windows.

"No thanks. I'm calling it an early night. I want to relax. Do you mind if I keep the fire going?"

"No, not at all. There's food upstairs. The diner's good for a meal, and they deliver. Tell them to put it on my tab if you order something."

Olivia hugged her aunt. "Thank you."

"We'll be staying at our house while you're here so you can have the upstairs apartment to yourself."

"Thanks again." Olivia locked the door behind her aunt.

She threw on a log and stoked the embers. She held her hands in front of her and watched the flames through her splayed fingers before sitting back in the chair.

An image of Max standing at the water's edge on the beach played in her mind. She smiled at the thought of being near him.

She woke up stiff from falling asleep in the armchair. A chill grabbed hold because the fire had turned to ash. The store was eerie without lights and all those old books on the shelves. No smell of coffee so, her aunt was still at home.

She rushed through a hot shower and got dressed.

Her stomach ached from hunger. The last thing she remembered having was hot chocolate. She found a piece of paper by the phone on the counter and left a note for her aunt.

She slipped out the back door.

"Awww, hello kitty." The cat ran away before she could pet it.

The sun breached the horizon and she couldn't remember the last time she'd been awake this early, never mind outside. The dings of the buoys in the marina clanged in unison. Seagulls swooped down near her feet.

"I guess you're not afraid of people." She laughed.

She walked up one side of Main Street and crossed to the other side. The stillness along the business district was comforting. No snow this morning and she'd remembered to wear her boots. Corky's was the only business open and she opted for hot chocolate instead of coffee. She must have been early because not even the fishermen were in the store. She grabbed a buttered roll to curb her hunger.

She stopped at a lamppost decorated with a wreath framing the globe. Her town didn't have a sense of community like Havenport did. She felt like she belonged here. She couldn't explain it other than she felt welcome and it was a nice feeling to have.

School was on her mind and she needed a break from thinking about it. Her aunt spent most of the previous night trying to convince her to go back after winter break but that wasn't the direction her heart took her.

She tossed her empty cup in the trashcan and stood at the head of the ramp looking out over the ocean. She strained to see a figure in the distance. *Is it?*

She squinted to get a better view. Damn, she'd forgotten to put in her contacts. She edged closer. *It's him.* She paced a few feet not knowing what to do. *I've got to.* She finger combed her hair and went onto the beach. His back was to her. She slowly walked up to him not wanting to startle him.

"Max?"

He must not have heard her.

"Max? Is that you?"

She walked closer and waited for him to turn around. He had to know she was there. He must have heard her the second time.

He reached down and grabbed a handful of sand and let it fall through his fingers.

"No shells." His voice filled with disappointment. He flicked his hand and rubbed it dry on his jeans.

She kept her smile from giving away her excitement at seeing him.

"Good morning. I see your boots dried out." She gritted her teeth to keep from saying something stupid again.

"Yeah. I stayed in so they could dry out. I didn't

have another pair with me." He stood with his back to her while he looked out into the horizon.

That must be the secret to dealing with him. He only talks in the morning. Great, she wasn't a morning person. This wasn't going to be easy. She walked around to his side.

"Looking for something special out there? A whale? A dolphin? Answer to something that you can't find anywhere else?"

"Maybe." He picked up a pebble and flung it into the water.

"So this is the first time you've seen the ocean?"

"No. Yesterday was."

"Right. Wet boots. I remember. I'm barely awake so I'll apologize now for any stupid questions or remarks I make." She put her hands in her pockets and watched the water lap at the tips of her boots.

"How long have you been living here?" He looked at her when he asked. His eyes glistened even more in the sunlight if that were possible.

"I don't. My aunt and uncle do. They live here and own the bookstore."

"I like that place."

"Yeah, it's cute. Too bad they're closing it."

"Why?"

"Moving to Florida. They're tired of the New England winters."

He looked around as if assessing what she said. "It doesn't seem too bad. Pennsylvania, now that place has some wicked winters. This is like springtime to me."

"Except for the waves and seagulls." She laughed.

"Yeah." He smiled.

"Damn, I got you to smile. I didn't know what to make of you. You're a hard man to talk to." She unzipped her jacket, it was warmer than she expected or maybe it was her present company who made her warm.

"I've been known to smile on occasion. I'm not used to strangers. Everyone knows you when you grow up in a small town."

She caught a sadness in his eyes. "What brought you here? It couldn't be the ocean in December. June or July would have been a better time of year to visit."

He put down his head and turned away.

She thought he was going to leave. Had she said something wrong? Damn, what was the matter with her? She was a social misfit. She reached out to him and gently held his elbow.

"Hey. I'm sorry if I said something wrong. I warned you that I'm not very good first thing in the morning."

He turned to her. "No, you didn't do anything wrong. I—never talk about this." He hesitated and took a deep breath. "I'm here to find out what I can about my birth parents. I was given up for adoption at birth and I got some information that led me here."

She didn't know what to say.

"I'm sorry. I didn't mean to intrude."

"Forget it. I mean I'd have to tell someone at some point if I'm going to find out anything about them."

He looked at her and her heart melted. She'd never known anyone who was adopted. Even though her father left she still knew him. Maybe she didn't see him as much as she wanted to, but there were signs that he was involved in her life. Even if it was just a check that arrived each month so that she didn't have a college tuition bill.

"I can help you," she blurted. Warmth spread through her chest and she filled with purpose. Yes, she wanted to help him. She'd always been good solving mysteries and enjoyed the challenge.

"Really? I'd appreciate that." He smiled.

She didn't have information, but her aunt or uncle must be able to help.

"I'll see what I can do. Give me your phone number so I can give it to my aunt." She dug into her purse and handed him a wrinkled receipt and pen.

He jotted down the digits and gave the paper back to her. "Thanks."

❄ ❄ ❄

They left the beach and walked along Main Street. Merchants arrived to open their stores for the day. She wasn't missing home much and thought she'd stay longer than the week she'd originally planned.

She watched Max from the corner of her eye while they strolled the cobblestone streets. He seemed a little more relaxed but still wasn't very talkative and that made her nervous. She couldn't pry into his past—that would be too forward. Or would it?

"What do you want to do today?" She spun in front of Max and walked backwards reading his face for an inclination.

"I haven't—stop you're going to fall or something." He grabbed her arm and kept her from stepping off the curb.

"I would've made it." She smiled at the strong hand clasped around the bend of her arm. Even through the jacket, she felt his strength.

"I don't need you getting hurt."

"Yes, sir." She saluted him with a sharp snap of her wrist. "So, continue."

"I haven't given it much thought. I really didn't have a

plan other than to come here and find out what I could."

Her heart softened. She couldn't imagine having to give up a child or being that child searching for biological parents. She thought about mom, who was due to arrive in a few hours. Their relationship wasn't the best, but they had one, and at that moment she realized how grateful she was to have her mother. In spite of their differences, her mother had always been there for her. She couldn't imagine living any other way.

"I told you that my aunt may be able to help."

"I thought about that and I'm not sure I want to start asking strangers about what little I know."

She slipped her arm through his and held him back.

"You have to start somewhere." She looked into his eyes and smiled.

"I know but I'm not ready."

She started to walk slowly still with her arm laced through his. "Then why did you come?"

"It was a spur of the moment thing. No planning went into this." He stopped and pulled them into a doorway to get out of the wind.

It was obvious he was hesitating.

She waited for him to make the next move. Surprisingly, she felt comfortable. Maybe it was his abrupt, yet polite disposition that sat well with her. Inspite of his inability to express himself with a little more than a few words, she was drawn to him and she wanted to know him better.

"Um, do you have a minute? This is my place and I need to get something."

She needed a restroom and felt weird to ask if she could go up to his place but she was too far from her aunt's store.

"Do you mind if I go up with you?" She subtly danced in place.

He looked surprised. "No, not at all. You're welcome. I was going to ask so you could get out of the wind, but I didn't know if that would be okay with you."

"Waiting would not be okay." She ran up the stairs, urgency trumping embarrassment. What a way to make a first impression. Oh well, she would be going home soon anyway. And who knew how long he planned on staying in town? His apartment was located above the bagel shop and the smell of garlic and onion filled the hallway. The stench infiltrated the apartment.

He followed behind her. She waited at the top of the staircase for him to open the door.

"Just walk in." He was about five steps behind her.

"You don't lock—" She turned the knob and the door opened. "I guess not." She found the bathroom and freshened up. Feeling much better she checked her teeth for stuck poppy seeds. Good to go. She found a travel bottle of mouthwash, swooshed some in her mouth and spit it out. She poured some water into the bottle so he wouldn't know she'd used his stuff.

She came into the living room. He was sitting on the couch looking through papers

"Thanks. I'm not in the habit of using strangers' bathrooms."

"No problem. Heck, back home it's not uncommon to find a neighbor sleeping in your bed."

Her eyes bolted wide. "What?"

He laughed. "Yeah, we don't lock the doors and sometimes, especially if the weather's bad, a neighbor may need to use your place for heat or just to get away from the wife."

"You talk like that happens a lot." She laughed.

"It depends on who your neighbor is." He smiled.

She sat back and slipped off her jacket. "It sounds like you come from a different world."

"I doubt it. I think people are the same, just talk differently." He shrugged.

She scanned his place and figured most of the furnishings came with the apartment. She doubted that he'd brought the weathered front porch rocking chair or the lobster trap and buoy bell. From what she saw, his belongings consisted of the duffel bag tossed in the corner and the beat up box that had a ton of papers in it.

"Can I help you with anything?"

"Not sure where to start." He scratched his head. "I had these in some type of order but things have lost their place from going in and out of the files."

She softly touched his hand and pulled it away from the box. She'd always had an interest in people's stories and his reeked of promise.

"How about you start at the beginning? I mean, you don't have to tell me anything if you don't want to, but I'm here to help and listen if you want to tell me. I've been told that I'm a good listener."

She loosened her grip on his hand and sat back. "Do you have anything to drink?"

"There's water from the sink, there might be some ice cubes. And beer."

"I'll take the water." She wrinkled her nose. She detested beer. "I'll get it."

"I'll have a beer. Thanks."

Her nosiness was itching to look behind the doors. That's why she offered to get the drinks in the first place. It was easy to find the small kitchen. The apartment couldn't have been more than three rooms. Kitchen, living room, and a bedroom. She couldn't get a thorough account because most of the doors were closed so she guessed.

She returned with the drinks. Max had taken off his jacket and boots. She guessed that he was comfortable with her being there. She sat a comfortable distance. Close enough to sense him, but not too close to be annoying.

"How long have you been here?" She sipped her water.

"Only a few days. I had a break in work so I thought I'd take the time to come out here. My company closes down the last two weeks of the year to change out conveyor belts and perform maintenance on the equipment. I rented the place for six months. It's cheaper than staying at a hotel and I can come back and forth when I want."

Hmm, so he'll be around.

"What kind of company do you work for?"

"Lumber mill."

"Hmm, that's different. I would have taken you for a mechanic or something like that. Not a lumberjack."

He laughed. "No, I don't cut down the trees, just process them once they get to us. Enough about that. I'm sure you don't want to hear about my boring life in Pennsylvania."

"You're right. I want to hear about what brought you here and what I'm going to be helping you with."

"You can start by helping me get this paperwork in date order."

She took a pile and scanned the contents without being obvious that she was reading the details. *Given up at birth.* She knew that. She rethought her strategy and worked on arranging the information and then she could throw questions at him.

He emptied his beer with one swallow.

Drinking in the morning was a sign her mother told her to watch out for when dating a guy. But this was an unusual circumstance so she was granting Max a pass. It must be upsetting to be so close yet so far with a search like this.

She leaned in front of him to wipe the water ring from the table and felt his breath on her neck. The hairs tingled from the warmth. She leaned in a little closer not sure what to make of what was going on.

His cheek moved closer to her, and he cupped her chin, and kissed her.

She didn't pull away but was cautious just the same. Maybe this is what her mother meant about beer so early in the day.

Max released his kiss and looked into her eyes. "Thank you for helping me with this."

She stood up and haphazardly pulled on her jacket. "I have to go help my aunt today. See you later?"

"I didn't mean to—"

"Gotta go." She ran down the stairs and out onto the street with her jacket open and flapping in the wind. Her cheeks hurt from smiling.

❄ ❄ ❄

"We have a lot going on today." Aunt Susan rushed around the store straightening books and dusting shelves.

"I'll check on the coffee and cookies." Olivia ate a brownie to make sure they tasted okay. Satisfied with the treat, she ate another one. She wasn't worried about putting on the pounds this week. It's Christmas time and, oh what the hell, she wanted to enjoy herself. She'd have all of January to work it off.

She straightened the small group of chairs and made sure the path to the book signing table was clear. She'd never heard of JD Watson, Beth Alexander, or Winnie Boyle but her aunt was excited about the event. And judging by the inquiries they'd received earlier that week, so were a lot of women.

"Look, people are lining up outside." Olivia pointed to the window.

"I know. I had people here first thing this morning and I told them they couldn't crowd the store. I didn't want regular customers scared away." Aunt Susan straightened the tinsel on the tree.

"I spent most of yesterday walking around. This is a nice place to be this time of year."

The doorbell interrupted. "Merry Christmas."

She flinched. She knew that voice without having to turn around.

"Patty, it's so good to see you." Aunt Susan ran to Olivia's mother and hugged her.

She poured Mom a cup of coffee and handed it to her. Best to get this done. "Hi, Mom. How was your trip?"

Patty unbuttoned her coat but left it on. "Fine. I'm not staying. Something came up and I have just enough time to stop in and say hi."

"Seriously? I thought you were spending the holiday in Havenport." Olivia poured herself a cup of coffee to steady her hands.

"I was but a job offer came up and it's in Boston. I don't have to tell you how excited that makes me, do I?"

No, Mom didn't. All their life that's all she ever heard. What a great place Boston is. They should move to Boston. Boston, Boston, Boston.

"So you won't be here for Christmas day?"

Patty hugged Olivia. "Well, honey, that depends on how the interview goes. I know you've been looking forward to this but...wait, how about I take you to lunch?"

"I promised Aunt Susan I would help with the author event."

Aunt Susan waved her away. "Don't worry, dear. Everything is set up and Marcie will be coming in to help with the register. You've done enough for today."

"You sure?" Olivia was uncertain.

"Absolutely. Enjoy yourself. Patty, I hope to see you on the return trip." Susan hugged her.

"I'm sorry to change plans at the last minute, but I really can't pass on this opportunity."

"I understand."

"Thanks, Aunt Susan. I'll clean up after the event so you can go home." She could use some alone time anyway. Life in the dorm had taken its toll on her, being around people all the time. She loved her aunt, but she really wanted to be alone for a bit. Aunt Susan nodded and went about her business.

"Isn't this a lovely town?" Patty slipped her arm through Olivia's.

"Yeah, it is. What are you in the mood for? It's not like there's a big selection." She squeezed her mother's hand.

She weighed her options. *Tell her now? Wait?*

"A burger is fine."

"Good, there's that small diner type cafe thing on the next corner."

The streets were busier than when she got there. With Christmas less than a week away, people must have been getting the last of their shopping done. She glanced up at Max's apartment. She didn't think he was that type of guy. To come out and kiss her like that—unexpected—it threw her off balance, though she liked it.

"Here it is." She opened the door and let Mom walk in first. The diner reminded her of a soda fountain shop she'd seen in an old black and white movie. If it weren't for the ocean the entire town could pass for a Frank Capra movie. The pace felt slower and she liked that. She didn't know if she could tolerate it every day, but for now it suited her.

"What an adorable place. Look, the booths are covered in red glitter vinyl like they used to be in the '50s."

"Um, Mom. Before you get too comfortable, there's something I have to tell you."

"What can I get you?" A waitress not much older than Mom took their order.

"Two burgers with fries," Olivia said.

"Soda?"

"No, seltzer with lime," Patty said.

"Have to save calories somewhere, huh?" The waitress smiled and left the table.

"What's so important that you need to tell me before I can eat my lunch?" Patty took off her coat and shoved it into the end of the booth.

Olivia thought she should leave her coat on in case she had to make a quick exit if Mom started a scene. Not that she was predisposed to them but telling Mom she didn't want to go back to school might be enough ammunition to start one.

"Mom, I've been doing a lot of thinking." She reached across the table and held her mother's hands.

"Oh, this is going to be big." Patty laughed.

Olivia could never fool her. It was moments like this that she realized how connected they were.

"I'm not returning to school." There, she got it out. No more knots in her stomach. She let out a huge sigh of relief.

Mom slid her hands from Olivia's grip and sat back.

"That's it?"

"Ah, yeah." She wrinkled her nose.

"Nothing more?"

"No, isn't that enough?"

"I suppose, but it doesn't surprise me." Patty crossed her arms.

"I expected you to flip out on me and scream."

"When have I ever screamed?" Patty took a french fry.

Olivia wasn't prepared for the carefree attitude. Could this be a trap? Mom had been in a better mood the last few months so maybe it had something to do with that.

"No, but I know how important this was to you."

"True, but I also know that you can't force something that's not there. I learned that the hard way from your father. Maybe you need to take a break. You can always go back. Right?"

Olivia nodded. That's exactly what she thought. Her breathing eased up now that she had that out of the way.

They caught up and walked to the bookstore. "I'm so glad you came and I could be honest with you. I was worried you'd be upset."

She opened the car door for her mom.

"Take off the next semester. Maybe college isn't right for you. I just want you to be happy. Who knows, maybe we'll both end up moving to Boston," Mom hugged her and drove away.

Happy that everything turned out fine, she turned in for the night.

❄ ❄ ❄

A snowplow jerked her out of her sleep. She got her bearings and glanced at the clock happy to find out it wasn't as late as she expected. Monday had been spent by herself since her aunt kept the bookstore closed because of the storm.

She got out of bed and searched the night table for the book she'd started reading during her last visit. It had to be hidden somewhere in the room. Her aunt didn't believe in putting a television in bedrooms, not even the guest room. Nothing in the drawer except for stationary that must have been there for years considering the yellowed edges.

She glanced out the window. The street glistened and white lights on the lamppost wreaths glowed beneath the mounds of snow that had landed on them. *A winter wonderland.*

She rummaged through a closet but only extra blankets and pillows filled the small space. It was too early to go back to sleep. A small wooden box sat on the roll-top desk. *I couldn't.* It wasn't like her to snoop but her aunt wouldn't put anything of value in a guest room. She pushed open the top of the box, feeling like she wasn't really searching through her aunt's private stuff.

Letters filled the box and she instantly recognized the stationary. Her grandmother had used the same design for as long as Olivia remembered. Her heart tugged and she wanted to read them, but couldn't. Those were secrets between her grandmother and her Aunt Susan. Seeing her grandmother's delicate script handwriting made her smile. She closed the box and left the secrets alone.

"What the?" she whispered.

Something was wrong. She pulled her robe belt tight around her waist and walked to the door. Voices. She wasn't alone. She closed her eyes and listened through the keyhole. Maybe it was the wind from the storm. She squeezed her eyes tighter to hear better. Rustling, and the low timber of a man and woman speaking in soft tones.

Her breath stilled. The last thing she wanted to do was bring attention to the fact that she was there. Who would break into a bookstore? *Don't panic.* She breathed in a slow steady motion, just enough to keep from getting light headed. *Where's the phone? None. Damn.* Her aunt must have taken it out.

She slinked over to her purse and pulled out her cell and wrapped her robe around it to muffle the sounds of the keypad and dialed 9-1-1.

"Hello, Havenport Precinct."

"There's someone in the Final Chapter Bookstore," she whispered.

"Sorry, miss. Can't hear you."

"Bookstore. Someone broke in. I'm by myself."

"Okay miss. We'll get someone there."

She waited by the window, straining to hear if the burglars were still there. She wasn't about to find out herself.

The clock ticked by, minutes seemed like hours.

A patrol car inched up to the store and she breathed easier but wasn't going downstairs until she knew it was safe. She cracked the door slightly.

Beams of light bounced around the walls.

"Hello, miss?"

The voice sounded official. She opened the door a little wider.

Footsteps headed her way.

She closed the door.

A soft knock jarred her.

"Miss?" A police officer pushed open the door.

Finally, she could breathe.

"Thank you. Did you get them?"

The flashlight blinded her. She flipped on the wall switch.

"There's no one down there. The back door was open, but it's old and maybe the latch didn't catch."

She knew what she'd heard. There had definitely been a man and a woman down there. "You sure?"

"Yep, nothing is disturbed. Just an open door. I'll check with you before we leave."

They walked down to the bookstore. Everything seemed okay. No broken glass. Nothing out of place.

The policeman was nice enough to check the upstairs rooms also. Nothing was there.

"Thank you. I'm sorry to have bothered you on this stormy night."

"Our pleasure, miss. Lock up and keep warm. Good night."

She double checked the back door. One last sweep around the store before going back to bed.

She didn't want to bother her aunt with the news of police coming to the store but she needed to talk to someone until she felt safe.

Snow came down fast. She sat near the fireplace, the flames down to a few hot coals, but it was still inviting.

She dialed Max's phone number. One ring and she hung up. *What do I say?* She dialed his number again.

"Hello?"

She didn't respond. *What's wrong with me?*

"Hello? Who's this?"

"Olivia."

She sensed hesitation on his end. Maybe he didn't like that she called.

"I want to apologize if I came across as too forward when I kissed you. I didn't mean to be."

"That was weird when you did that."

"I know. It was for me too. I'm not sure what came over me. Can we start over?"

He sounded sincere. She did feel a connection when they were together and maybe he did too.

"Sure." His voice made her feel safe. She curled up

in the storefront window and looked down the street at his apartment.

"It's a pretty night, isn't it?" he said.

"Yeah, it is." Her eyes were closing. "All of a sudden I'm exhausted. I need to get to bed. Can we pick up this conversation later?"

"Sure. Have a good night. Talk to you soon."

"Good night." She hung up the phone and watched the snow fall.

❄ ❄ ❄

She missed Max. He hadn't called and she didn't want to come across as eager. She used the time to help her sort through her dilemma of whether or not to return to school. Her mother's reaction made her think twice. It wasn't unusual for Mom to use reverse psychology on her. At first she thought that was the tactic, but realized it wasn't as she thought more about it. The divorce had changed her mother. She'd become tolerant and easy going after the initial onslaught of anger had subsided. But Olivia never thought that thinking would extend to her college plan.

Aunt Susan did what she could to get information for Max but Olivia wasn't sure how helpful what she found out would be for him. She dialed his number.

"Hello?"

He sounded tired. Was it too early to call? Too late?

"Good after nearly noon." She laughed. "Can you meet me for coffee at the corner cafe?"

He yawned into the phone. *I must have woken him.*

"Give me about fifteen minutes. I'll meet you there."

"Okay. See you in a few."

She took her time maneuvering around the snow while she walked to the corner diner. She was starving. A cold wind blew past her and reminded her that the ocean was behind her. She thought back to the day she first met Max and how he wanted to see the ocean no matter how cold it was. She realized how she took things like that for granted. It never occurred to her that life was different for people who weren't from the north east. She realized she'd have to be patient with people, not everyone thought like her.

She got to the diner before Max and ordered her food. Hunger took precedence over any good deed right now.

"Burger, fries, and cole slaw, please. Oh, and a fountain root beer." she said to the waitress before she even got to her booth. Mom wasn't there to lecture her on the evils of soda and it just seemed to belong with the food she ordered.

The door opened and a few more people came in, one of them being Max. She smiled, hoping she didn't appear silly. She wasn't good at this guy stuff and especially after he'd kissed her in his apartment. *Play it cool.* She waved him over.

"Hello." He sat across from her in the booth.

"I've already ordered. Starving, not being rude." She slid the ketchup bottle toward her and twirled it between her index finger and thumb.

"I'll just have coffee. I ate this morning."

He kept his jacket on. She got the impression he didn't plan on staying. The waitress set down Olivia's food and Max's coffee.

"Come here so much that the waitress knows what you want?"

He laughed. "A bit. I was here for breakfast and I

don't each lunch this early. So yeah, you could say she has me figured out."

"Well I'm eating." She doused her burger and fries with ketchup. "Yum."

He leaned forward and sipped his coffee.

She wondered what he was thinking and the quietness made her nervous.

"I don't know if what my aunt found will help. She said the name was familiar but it could be something she heard in passing."

"I'd appreciate anything. I know it's a long-shot but any piece of information could lead to who my parents are."

She slid a folded piece of paper across the table to him like she was sneaking a trade secret and didn't want anyone to see. He took it from her, but resisted opening the note.

"You don't want to see what's in it?" She finished her last ketchup soaked fry.

"Of course I do."

"Well?"

He sat back and slowly unfolded the paper. His eyes narrowed and he looked confused.

"Library." He held the paper toward her.

"Yeah, that was the best my aunt could do. She said to speak to Selma at the library. She's lived here a long time and if anyone would know your parents, it would be her. I know it's not much, but it could turn out to be something."

"I guess." He folded up the paper and put it in his jean pocket.

"I'll go with you if you want." And she meant it. She wasn't feeling sorry for him. She gently nudged his leg with her foot. Now she was being forward but she couldn't help it. There was something about him that drew her in. Maybe that's what he felt the other night.

"It might be worth a shot before I leave town." He slid out from the booth.

"What do you mean, leave town?" She slid out of the booth and grabbed his elbow.

"I was thinking the other night that this could be the wrong way to go about finding my biological parents. I mean, what if I find them and they don't want to be found?"

She slid her hand into his and escorted him to the register to pay the check.

"This isn't the place to discuss this." They went outside. The sun was bright and the wind calm.

"The snow doesn't last long around here, does it?" he said.

"No, the salt air gets rid of it pretty fast. Here. Sit." She pulled him to a bench in front of Wags and Walks.

"Cute name for a dog groomer." He leaned back to look at the sign.

"That's what this town is all about. Cute. A few blocks away and you get away from cute and move into mega rich." She laughed.

He rested his head on the back of the bench, looking up at the sky.

"You know, I came here full of enthusiasm and determination to find them. It never occurred to me that they probably don't want to know me. I mean they did give me away."

Her heart pounded. She remembered the pain she felt when her father left. No explanation and he was out of the house. She hadn't been able to make sense of her world turned upside down. The hurt Max lived with every day—well, she couldn't even begin to imagine the pain.

She wrapped her arms around him and rested her head on his chest.

"Listen, I know none of this is my business but you're here. You came here for a reason and it would be a shame if you left before you even tried to connect with something that would minimize the pain."

She rested her hand on his and lightly squeezed his fingers. Her pulse quickened—he looked into her eyes.

"Thank you." He opened his hand and held hers.

She was hooked.

❄ ❄ ❄

"Merry Christmas!" Aunt Susan rapped on the bookstore door. Her arms were loaded with presents that were ready to crash to the ground if she moved an inch the wrong way.

Olivia let her aunt and uncle in. They'd decided to spend the holiday in the bookstore so they could watch the town festivities from the warmth of the fireplace and be away from the crowds.

"This is the day we get the most traffic. People from other neighborhoods drive by the decorated mansions and then they have to drive by the water and back through Main Street to see if something's going on." Aunt Susan dropped the pile of gifts on the table next to the coffee and snack setup.

Olivia had finally figured out how to make coffee and surprised her aunt and uncle with breakfast holiday treats from the local bakery. There was a chance Mom could make it today from Boston but she wasn't getting her hopes up.

"They're gathering around the town square clock. We snuck in just in time. I'm not standing in the weather, singing until my tonsils freeze from the cold." Uncle Matthew poured a cup of coffee and sat in a rocking chair that was just for him when he visited the store. He would settle in sipping his coffee, watch the carolers, and then fall asleep.

She had a short window of quiet to have a conversation with her aunt before her uncle started snoring so loudly the windows shook.

"I've made a decision about school. I'm not going back, at least not right now. Why waste money and time when I don't even know what I want to be for the rest of my life?"

Aunt Susan took a seat at the table with Olivia. Her aunt reached out and squeezed Olivia's hand. "I do understand that and it does make sense. I'm just afraid you'll never go back. That's why I've been struggling with getting rid of my bookstore."

"You're selling it, aren't you?" Olivia loaded a napkin with dainty cinnamon crumb cakes, and a bite-size pound cake topped with cream and a strawberry.

"Yes, we were selling." Uncle Matthew blurted and returned to people watching through the window. "You know, we could see better if we moved that tree."

"The tree stays where it is. Just ignore him." Susan flicked her hand like he would vanish at her will.

"We've decided to leave the store to you. I can't promise what future it holds because business has not been good. But the building is paid for so there's no mortgage, only taxes."

Olivia choked on her strawberry. "I can't accept that."

"Of course you can." Uncle Matthew said without taking his eyes off the townspeople gathering in front of the store. "We never should have put those benches out there."

Aunt Susan ignored him and continued. "I've told you many times that you are like the daughter we never had. Of course we would leave it to you."

"If you want to leave it to me in your will, I get it, but not now."

"Of course now. Why wait until we're gone? Once we leave, we won't have any use for it. I'd like you to enjoy it while we're still around to see you taking care of it."

"What about your house?" She didn't mean to sound greedy, she simply wanted to know how much she was expected to take care of. It was overwhelming just thinking about the bookstore. She didn't have any experience and wouldn't know the first thing to do. Hell, she'd only learned to make coffee this morning, and she was sure running a bookstore was more involved than having a fresh pot of java ready every few hours.

"We're selling that, so don't worry. We think the apartment upstairs is roomy enough for one person. It has everything you need, even the small guest room."

Ah, the room where she'd stood terrorized as robber ghosts shopped. She didn't care what the police officer said. She knew what she'd heard. Without witnesses, it was her story. The first thing she'd do was get that back door lock fixed.

"There's one condition." Aunt Susan folded her arms and sat straight.

"Of course there is." Olivia laughed. That was her family's way and her aunt and uncle were very much like her grandparents, Emily and Michael Chadwick. After all, Aunt Susan and Emily were best friends and Uncle Matthew and Michael were brothers, so there was an unbreakable bond.

"And I'm serious about this. You must finish school. I'll agree to you taking off a year to figure out what you want to do, but the title to this place stays in trust for you until you graduate and I don't mean from a community college. It you want to start there and transfer to a four year college, that's fine."

"What happens to the store if I don't graduate?"

"Easy, you don't get the store. I've given instructions to our attorney. You have five years to complete your degree from the day you start, which can be no later than one year of finding yourself, which starts now."

"Can I make changes to the business?" She was excited and scared. Her mind raced with visions of adding new merchandise while retaining as much of the old as she could.

"Of course you can, but I ask that you always have the town culture in mind when doing so."

A rapid knock on the door stopped their conversation.

Max paced back and forth until Olivia let him in.

"I'm not staying. I wanted to say goodbye to you before I leave and head home for Pennsy."

She grabbed the front of his jacket and pulled him into the store. "You can't leave. Apparently, none of us can. Well except for those two." She held her hand out as if introducing her aunt and uncle.

"They're leaving me. Leaving me here to run this store, while they unload everything and move to Florida because they like flamingos better than snow."

Max shoved his hands in his jean pockets with a blank stare on his face. She didn't know him well enough yet, but he was someone she wanted to know and she wasn't letting him go so easily.

"That's great, I guess, right? This is good for you?"

"It's wonderful, but I'm going to need someone to help me out with fixing a few things around here but most of all—someone to listen to me whine when it's obvious that I'm in over my head and don't know what I'm doing."

"And you assume that I know how to fix stuff?"

"Raised on a farm?"

"Yes."

"You know how to fix stuff. You can start with the back door lock."

He walked to the rear of the store.

"Hey, wait. I didn't..."

She followed him to the broken lock and he played with the catch. "Hey, I didn't mean for you to start now. It's Christmas! Come on, let's spend some time getting to know each other. My family doesn't bite and you never know what might be discovered."

He smiled. His smile and spark in his eyes told her he wanted to be there with her, maybe not for forever but at least until the end of his vacation.

"Hey, I think I know what can make you want to stay a while."

"What's that?"

She raised her hands and held his face. Her fingers played with his soft stubble. Yep, there was definitely a connection and no way was she letting him leave town until they discovered what it was about. She slid her hands up behind his neck and pulled him into her.

This time it was her decision, and he wasn't pulling away.

"I could be convinced to stay a little longer." He smiled. "You know, just in case I get a lead on my parents or something."

He leaned into her.

"Or something." She held him tight. There was no denying the energy pulsing through her veins.

Her lips left his and she whispered. "See, you never know what you'll discover. It just takes time. Merry Christmas, Max Porter."

Want to know the special meaning behind the ornament Olivia Baxter hangs on the Christmas tree in The Final Chapter bookstore? Find out how her grandmother, Emily, and her Aunt Susan competed for the heart of the same man in CHRISTMAS SPIRITS—available in TIMELESS KEEPSAKES: A Collection of Christmas Stories.

About the Author

LITA HARRIS spends her time between New Jersey and the Endless Mountains region of Pennsylvania, where she writes most of her books. She also lived in Alaska for a short time just for fun. An avid crafter, unused supplies clutter her basement and attempts at making pottery, jewelry, and stained glass are proudly displayed in her house, usually behind a picture or holding a door open. She also makes candles and homemade soap. With enough books to stock a small library she may need to construct a building to store her literary obsessions.

She writes in multiple genres, including women's fiction, contemporary romance, paranormal, and cozy mysteries.

❊ ❊ ❊

For more information about Lita, please visit her website at www.LitaHarris.com or at Twitter.com/LitaHarris and Facebook.com/LitaHarrisAuthor.

Also by Lita Harris

Love at Christmas

Kristen Anderson and Luke Baldwin discover a family secret on Christmas Eve that threatens their love for one another.

What will the holiday bring them?

❄ ❄ ❄

<u>Timeless Tales – Short Stories</u>

Christmas Spirits featured in Timeless Keepsakes (Christmas Spirits is also available separately)

Chasing Fireflies featured in Timeless Escapes

Trusting Kindness featured in Timeless Treasures

Till Death Do Us Part featured in Timeless Vows

❄ ❄ ❄

<u>Havenport – Novellas</u>

New Beginnings featured in Welcome to Havenport

Kindred Spirits featured in Haunted Havenport

Snowbound in Havenport — Fall, 2017

❄ ❄ ❄

Baby, It's Cold Outside

Emma Kaye

❄ ❄ ❄

Jane Caulfield should have known better than to read aloud from a book of magick during her famous sister-in-law's book signing at The Final Chapter bookstore. After all, the last spell she cast brought her and her brother forward in time two hundred years. She knows the power of magick.

She didn't know the spell would bring her nineteenth century love, Adam Royce, forward in time. Or that he would assume he'd died and joined her in heaven. Jane gets more than she bargained for trying to persuade Adam they're both alive and in the twenty-first century.

Jane knows they're soul mates, but convincing Adam may not be so easy. Will Adam insist on returning to his own time, or can Jane use both love and a little magick to help him understand that this time and place is exactly where he's meant to be?

Dedicated to ~

My family. I love you.

The Scribes. It's hard to believe we're on our fifth Timeless book. It's been an amazing journey, and I'm so happy to have taken it with you all.

Baby, It's Cold Outside
by Emma Kaye

"I can't believe The Final Chapter's closing. This bookstore is one of my favorite places in Havenport." Jane Caulfield held open the door for her sister-in-law, while juggling a box full of bookmarks, postcards, and pens. The bell jingled overhead, announcing their arrival. Winnie hurried through, dropped her basket of home-made biscotti on the table set aside for signing authors, and ushered her two daughters inside.

"It's a shame. I used to come here all the time when I was growing up." Winnie cradled her pregnant belly with one hand and rubbed her back with the other. "Ooh, this one's a kicker." She laughed. "Holly and Rose weren't nearly this active."

Jane laid her hand lightly upon Winnie's side and laughed in delight as the baby pressed back against her palm. "Do you think it's a boy, then?"

Winnie shrugged. "Who knows? You know how

Bastian feels about finding out the sex ahead of time. We all just have to wait and see."

The two girls took off down one of the aisles. Jane shooed Winnie toward the register and said, "I'll get them. Bastian should be here any minute to pick them up. You go talk to the owner and get everything settled."

The girls weren't hard to find. She followed their giggles to the area in back devoted to children's books and a small selection of toys. Some of her fourth graders had their art projects proudly displayed along one wall.

"Auntie Jane, Auntie Jane!" Rose ran up to her, a stuffed unicorn in one hand, and a dragon in the other. "Play."

Jane took the dragon and spent the next few minutes playing pretend games with her beloved nieces. She couldn't get enough of the girls. With their father's bright blue eyes and their mom's golden blond hair, they were adorable. Jane enjoyed watching them twist her older brother around their little fingers.

Bastian arrived and the girls ran into his arms. He swung them into a bear hug and carried them over to Winnie for a big family embrace.

Jane tried to squash the wave of envy that washed over her. She didn't regret casting the spell that brought her and Bastian forward in time so he could be reunited with his one true love, Winnie. She'd do it again.

But she worried she'd never find a love of her own. Every once in a while, her thoughts dwelled on Adam Royce, the handsome sailor she'd met on the trip from London to the Caribbean right before they'd left 1818. What she wouldn't give to find out what had happened to him. Dead by now, obviously. She sighed.

He'd been so kind, she'd fallen head over heels for him by the time they'd reached land.

He hadn't returned her affections. On their last day

aboard, she'd discovered he'd only spent time with her because the captain had ordered him to keep her out of the rest of the crew's way.

"Jane?"

She hurried round the corner to spend the next half hour helping get ready for the signing. The parents of several of Jane's students stopped by to buy books and ask if they knew why the front window of Wags and Walks was boarded up. Everyone wanted to know what had happened and they'd all heard a different story. Everything from vandalism to a malfunctioning snow maker. Some people seemed more interested in how Mac MacDonald, the town's hottest volunteer firefighter, had seemed more interested in the owner's visiting sister than putting out the fire.

Jane met the other authors—Beth Alexander and JD Watson—but when JD took his seat next to Beth the tension between the two was palpable. After sharing a "What's that all about?" look with Winnie, Jane quietly went about her own business and ignored them. She'd see about getting her own signed copies at the end of the day.

Jane was proud of her sister-in-law. Winnie's "fictional" book about how she and Bastian had met had gotten her onto the best seller list and sparked a series of time travel romances readers loved. The third book had just launched and so far the reviews were fantastic.

Jane didn't envy her.

Not at all.

Liar.

Susan introduced Winnie first, so Jane listened for a few minutes before wandering over to the new age section to find a pack of tarot cards.

She picked up a lightly used deck. A wave of nausea rose up her throat. The cards dropped from her numbed fingers back onto the shelf. She grimaced and poked them back into place with the tip of her finger. The last owner must have been sick last time they'd been held. She could cleanse them, of course, but would rather not own a set with such sadness attached to them. She'd warn Susan, though. Maybe offer to cleanse the cards after Christmas.

An aged, dark brown leather book caught her eye. The gold lettering on the spine was faded to the point of illegibility. Something compelled her to pull it off the shelf. She fumbled, barely managing to rescue the book before it hit the floor. She caught the front cover and gripped it tight, wincing when one of the pages sliced against her finger.

She placed the open book on a conveniently placed side table and frowned at the smudge of blood she'd left on the page. Darn it. Her eyes drifted over the words.

On Bringing Forth True Love.

A spell book?

She turned to the cover, but the writing was as faded as the spine. She flipped through, the pages consistently falling open to the same page. A list of ingredients accompanied the words. Winnie would enjoy reading this. Maybe her readers would like to hear it. Could be fun. The words would hold no power without all the ingredients to hand.

Keeping her finger between the pages to mark her spot, she tucked the book under her arm and peeked around the corner to see how Winnie was doing. The lines had shortened considerably. Winnie chatted with a group of women huddled around the table while she signed their purchases.

Jane approached slowly, listening to the conversation to see if she'd have long to wait. The women peppered Winnie with questions.

"Where do you get your ideas? What kind of research did you do for *Tempting the Viscount*?"

Winnie fielded question after question, while Jane winced at the butchered pronunciation of Viscount. Only diehard Regency romance readers ever got it right. She wasn't about to correct one of Winnie's fans, though. "Perfect timing!" She stepped up to Winnie's side and waved the book at the women. "I was just bringing this to show Winnie."

Winnie leaned forward. "Ooh, what is it?"

The women looked on, a delighted gleam in their eyes.

Jane placed the opened book in front of Winnie with a flourish. "Love spells."

"Ooh," one of the women leaned across the table for a closer look. "Do they work?"

Jane gave a slight negative shake of her head to Winnie's inquiring look. Winnie, of all people, knew how well a spell could work when read by the right person. But Jane wasn't concerned. She had no intention of casting such a spell, and intent was extremely important when dealing with magick of this nature.

The consequences of conjuring for personal gain could be dire. The spells almost always went wrong, causing nothing but heartache for the witch who used them.

No. She wasn't using magick to find love. No matter how much she wished it were that simple.

"'On Bringing Forth True Love.'"

She paused to smile at the small group listening with rapt attention.

"'Bring to me, what I cannot see,
I have been blind, please set me free.

A love that's true, will stand through time,
I pledge my heart, my soul, my mind.
The one I seek, so shall I find.'"

An image of Adam flashed across her mind and filled her with longing. She pushed him from her thoughts as she continued reading the words, but that sense of desire couldn't be denied.

"'To one who'll love, and be with me,
I shall be true, so he shall see.
From where he dwells, so far, so vast,
Bring my love home from days gone past.'"

A shimmer of nerves skittered up her spine. Maybe reading this hadn't been such a great idea. But the ladies looked at her so expectantly, she gathered up her courage and finished the passage.

"'If it please, so mote it be.'"

Jane gasped as a rush of wind swirled around her. What the…?

"What was that?" Winnie whispered out of the corner of her mouth while smiling at the women before them.

"I don't know," she replied just as quietly so no one else would hear. "It's almost like the spell is working, but I don't have any of the ingredients so it shouldn't be possible."

Winnie pulled the book toward her. "Blood of the hopeful, sage, crystals—yellow jasper, clear quartz, etcetera,… Jane, have you actually looked around the shop?"

"Of course I have. I've been all over the place today."

Winnie pointed and Jane followed the direction of her finger toward the ceiling. "Oh." She clapped her hand over her mouth to squelch her yelp of surprise. Beautiful multi-colored crystals—was that yellow one jasper?—hung from the ceiling, creating a twinkling, fairylike canopy over their heads. Winnie coughed and the direction of her finger changed to flit about the room, pointing out small dishes filled with potpourri. Jane sniffed and caught a hint of—bloody hell—sage, among others. The ingredients for the spell surrounded them.

A wave of relief flooded through her. The personal contribution of the caster—that couldn't come from any shop and she hadn't given anything of herself.

Close call.

As Winnie went on to explain to the women how she would use something like this spell for inspiration for her own work, Jane stepped away to put the book back on the shelf.

A stinging sensation on her finger brought a weight crashing down in her stomach. She let the book fall open to the spell and glanced down at the brownish smudge of dried blood on the page. The last ingredient.

Blood of the hopeful.

❄ ❄ ❄

"Are you sure you wouldn't like to spend the night?"

"No. Thank you." Jane leaned back in through the window of Winnie's car, shaking off the dusting of snow already accumulating on her head. "I long for a hot bath and a good night's rest in my own bed."

"What about the spell? I thought for sure... I mean—I came right away when you cast a spell for Bastian. Shouldn't this have worked the same?"

"I would suspect so." *So why didn't it?*

"Any idea what happened?"

No. "One of the ingredients must have been missing. There was enough to cause the magick to gather, but not enough to complete the casting. No true love for me." She said it in a singsong voice, as if it were all a joke. She didn't manage to convince herself.

Winnie reached across the passenger seat to squeeze Jane's hand where it rested on the door. "That's not true, Jane. I know you gave up a lot for me and your brother. And it's been hard adjusting to life here. But you've done so well."

Jane nodded. She loved her life and had worked hard to earn what she'd made for herself: earning her degree, securing a position as an elementary school art teacher, buying a condo in town, and moving out on her own. She'd gained her independence. An impossibility in the early eighteen hundreds when she'd grown up.

She'd never imagined she could accomplish so much. Yet she had no one with which to share her wonderful life.

"There'll be love for you, too. I know it."

Jane fought back tears and returned Winnie's affection with a squeeze of her own. "Of course. I was jesting." *Liar.* When had the truth become such a difficult thing? She'd always been unfailingly honest. Today all she'd seemed to do was lie. Why could she not be honest about her fears?

Because she did not wish to become a burden to those she loved. Winnie and Bastian were so happy, she could not bear to put a damper on their joy. She forced a smile. "But not about wanting that bath. I do so enjoy my

Jacuzzi tub." She looked down the street at the thickly falling snow. A snowplow rumbled by, barely keeping up with the weather. "You should go before the storm worsens. Drive carefully Winnie, dear."

She jogged up the sidewalk, her breath fogging in the frigid air. Once she had the door unlocked, she turned to wave to Winnie in reassurance all was well.

Lighting candles and filling the tub took only a few minutes. She poured herself a healthy glass of merlot and placed it within reach of the tub. With the jets turned to full power, she slipped into the hot water with a sigh of bliss. She'd been in this century for eight years, but she still marveled at turning a knob and having a hot bath in moments. She'd always felt guilty putting her servants through the trouble of carting all those buckets of hot water up three flights of stairs from the kitchen fires to her chambers.

She took a small sip of wine, then placed the glass on the edge of the tub so she could submerge under the bubbling water. The music she'd put on faded as the water slid over her head. Such a romantic setting she'd set up. All for herself. Lovely.

Why hadn't the spell worked? Did it mean she would never be able to find love? Was she destined to spend the rest of her life alone?

Had casting such a spell for personal gain doomed her?

Because it should have worked. Even though she hadn't known it, all the ingredients had been there. She'd even been thinking about how much she wished she'd had a chance to make things work with Adam.

Her breath released in a rush when she came up for air. She shoved the wet hair out of her eyes and reached for her towel to wipe her face.

"Is this heaven?" a deep, British voice asked from less than a foot away.

She screamed. Her heart hammered against her ribs. Her glass crashed to the tile floor as she grabbed a towel and did her best to cover her nakedness. *9-1-1. 9-1-1. Where's my phone?*

How had he gotten in? What did he want? Who was he?

A figure knelt by her side, next to the towel bar. *Had he handed her the towel?* He tossed shards of glass into the garbage can and wiped up the wine with a hand towel.

He stood. The buff colored breeches, off-white linen shirt, and dark coat stopped her thoughts in mid panic. He was soaking wet. And those clothes. They weren't from this time. They were from...

She looked up, and up, into the stranger's face. He'd tower over her even if she were standing. She knew what it felt like to stand beside him. She'd done it before, looking over the rail into the ocean depths below. "Adam Royce?" Her voice came out on a squeak. Dreaming. She must be. The warmth of the bath had lulled her to sleep. She bit her lip, then winced at the pain.

Not dreaming.

His eyes wide, his mouth gaping open the tiniest bit, he looked as surprised as she felt. "You know me? I will admit, you look familiar, yet I do not believe we have met."

The roar of the jets almost drowned out his voice. She flipped the switch and the water stilled. Adam's eyes widened further, his gaze somewhere south of her face. She glanced down at herself and heat rushed to her cheeks. The towel had floated to the side of the tub, pushed by the jets no doubt, leaving her body exposed to his view. She struggled to pull the fabric to rights but soaked as it was, the towel refused to bend to her wishes.

"This is ridiculous." She grabbed another towel off the rack, flipping it open to use as a curtain while she exited the tub. Adam stared. "The polite thing would be to turn your back. This is highly improper."

"I'm dead. Being proper isn't my most immediate worry at the moment."

She snorted. "You're not dead." She tucked the towel around her while keeping a wary eye on him. Dead? "Whyever do you think so?"

"No other explanation." He ran a hand through the dark brown hair plastered to his skull. A leather tie clung to the remains of a ponytail. She remembered he'd always kept it tied back, but more often than not, his hair would fall forward anyway.

The scruffy beard was new.

She liked it. Gave him a rough, rugged look.

"There was a storm. The mast cracked, swept half the crew overboard when it crashed on deck. We were dead in the water after that. Wasn't long before a wave knocked her on her side. I was sent below to save passengers trapped below deck. Get them out. Give them a chance to survive the storm. Only…" His voice faded and his gaze slid from her into the distance.

She slipped into her robe while he was distracted. The thin silk clung to her limbs, but it was floor length and at least covered her better than the towel. "Only?" she prompted.

He shook his head, ran a hand along his jaw. "Only, I was trapped instead. The water rushed in, I couldn't… I heard the sweetest voice. I figured it was one of the passengers, though I couldn't recall any of them speaking in such angelic tones."

Had he heard her recite the spell? He must have. Excitement surged through her. She'd cast the spell and Adam, the man she'd loved back in her own time, had somehow answered her call. Had their time together meant more than the passing fancy of a young girl?

"The water rose and… I was here." He stared her in the eye. "The voice. That was you, wasn't it? Did you bring me here?"

She nodded. She should explain, but she couldn't make any sound come out of her mouth while she stared into his gorgeous hazel eyes. She'd gazed into them before, but while she'd felt passion and the youthful stirrings of love, he'd seen nothing more than a passenger with whom he'd been saddled. No. That wasn't entirely true. He'd recognized her infatuation and done his best to discourage it. Too old for her, he'd said.

"How old are you?" she asked.

His eyes widened, his eyebrows raised. She'd obviously surprised him with her question. He was too polite to ignore her though. He'd answer, even if it was none of her business.

"Eight and twenty."

A year older than when she'd known him. Exactly how much time had passed for him? Did it really matter? She was twenty-four now. Definitely old enough for him. She took a step closer.

He watched her approach with a question in his gaze. His glance flicked downward once. Twice. She could see the effort it took him to keep his eyes off her body. Power surged through her as she watched him struggle to be a gentleman. He'd overlooked her easily back then. Not anymore.

When she got within a foot of him, he held out a hand to keep her back.

She stopped, unsure what exactly she'd planned to do when she reached him. Suddenly self-conscious she tugged the belt of her robe tighter around her waist.

"How did you bring me here? And why? Are you an angel?"

"No. I'm not." She opened her linen closet and

pulled out the largest towel she owned. She doubted it would cover much of him at all. She'd remembered how tall he was, but having him near her again...she shivered. Her nipples puckered under the soft brush of silk when she inhaled. She crossed her arms across her chest to hide her reaction to him, and handed him the towel. Not easy while trying to keep her chest covered. "Why don't you dry off? I'll see if I have any of my brother's clothes for you to put on. When you're done, come into the living room and I'll explain everything."

How exactly was she going to do that? She dug a pair of Bastian's sweat pants and a t-shirt from the back of the closet and passed them to Adam. "Here you go."

He bowed and muttered his thanks.

She shut the door and ran to her room to get dressed. What in the world was he going to think when she told him what she'd done?

❄ ❄ ❄

Jane sat in a wingback chair near the fireplace. She dried her palms on her jeans for the umpteenth time. Perhaps she should have selected a dress? What did one wear when telling their true love he'd been transported through time against his will because she'd wanted to entertain a few women she didn't even know at a book signing? What should she say? She had to tell him something.

If he ever came out of the bathroom.

He was certainly taking his time. He'd been in there a good half hour now. What could he possibly be doing?

Rinnngggg.

She jumped as the telephone next to her let out a shrill

ring. Caller ID told her it was Winnie or Bastian. Should she let it continue? She wasn't in the mood to chat.

No. Bastian would be at her door within the next twenty minutes, despite the heavy snowfall. She snatched up the phone before it could go to voice mail.

"Hi, Jane. It's Winnie."

Jane sighed in relief. The knot in her stomach eased slightly. She loved her brother, but he wasn't always the easiest man to deal with. Overprotective didn't even begin to describe him. She could imagine how he'd respond to a finding out a man had appeared in her bathroom while she was naked.

"I got the feeling you were disappointed the spell didn't work. Did you consider that maybe it did, but that it takes a while? I mean, if your true love lives in—I don't know—Japan, or some other far away country, it could take a while for him to get here, ya know?"

Jane couldn't stop the laugh that burst from her mouth. "Oh, Winnie, dear. You have no idea."

"What do you mean?" Winnie lowered her voice, "What happened? Did it work? Did someone show up? Who is he? Is it someone you know?"

"You could say that." Jane told Winnie all about Adam showing up in her bathroom, stopping and starting when Winnie exclaimed or asked for more detail.

"Oh. My. God." Winnie's tone was almost comical. Jane could imagine the look of wonder on her sister-in-law's face.

"That about sums it up, yes."

"He's a good guy? Are you safe? Or should Bastian and I head over—or call the police?"

"He's a perfect gentleman. I got to know him quite well." She'd spent almost every waking hour for an entire month following him around aboard ship. "He would never harm me."

"If you're sure."

Jane made a reassuring sound. What was Winnie thinking? Would she tell Bastian? Tell him Jane needed rescuing? Or did she trust Jane's judgment?

Winnie continued, "I don't think I'll tell your brother about this quite yet."

"Thank you." Jane let out her breath in a gush. She had no plan as of yet, but at least she'd have a chance to make her own decision without Bastian's interference. "But what should I do? I'm waiting for him now. What should I say? Do I tell him the nature of the spell?"

"No! Absolutely not. He might freak out. You need to give him a chance to know you a little first. No one wants to be *told* who to love. If he is your soul mate that should come naturally."

"Then what do I say?"

The bathroom door squeaked open.

She gasped and whispered into the phone, "I must go. He's coming."

"Call me later."

Jane fumbled the phone into its holder as Adam sauntered down the hall. Her hands shook so badly she clutched them together in her lap to still them.

Bastian's old sweatpants gathered a good three inches above Adam's ankles. And the shirt. Good lord, the shirt clung to him like she wanted to.

Where had that thought come from?

From the rippling of his stomach muscles clearly outlined by the tightly stretched fabric of the tee shirt. Or from the way the sweatpants clung to his legs and ended ridiculously high, leaving a wide patch of skin from calf to bare feet. Or maybe from the wide smile on his handsome face.

"You have the most wondrous items in that room. Is everything one wants so readily available in heaven?"

Oh, no. He still thought he was in heaven. "This isn't heaven. You're not dead."

He sank onto the couch across from her. She'd always thought her sofa was large, but he dwarfed it to the point it looked smaller than a love seat.

"I must be. Had I survived the storm, I would not be witness to such wonders as you have here." He jumped up and approached her television. "What is this?" He ran his hand along the top of the flat screen.

The chiming of the TV turning on made Jane dive for the remote control. She quickly clicked the off button before the screen blazed to life. Television would be much too difficult to explain at the moment. She'd found it overwhelming when she first arrived.

Disaster averted, she placed a hand on Adam's arm. "Please, won't you have a seat? We need to discuss what's happening."

He turned his attention her way and her breath caught, they stood so close. He radiated heat better than the fire she'd started in her modern gas fireplace. He looked just as she remembered him, and the tingling breathlessness she'd always felt in his presence was exactly the same.

He frowned, his brow crinkling as he studied her face. "You are remarkably familiar. I feel as though I know you, yet cannot recall from where."

"We have met before." He remembered! A smile stretched her face wide. She struggled to control the giddiness his recognition caused. Surely she hadn't been entirely insignificant if she was familiar to him despite the passing of eight years and a wildly different setting. "I was a passenger on your ship. We spent quite a lot of time together."

He stepped closer, leaning his head down so they were eye to eye. She forced herself to keep breathing, though her lungs didn't seem to want to function properly. His breath was fresh, like he'd sampled her toothpaste while in the bathroom. Had he used her toothbrush? It seemed such an intimate item to share. If he were using her toothbrush, surely it was not completely improper to stand so close to him.

"I think I'd remember that, my lovely." He ran a finger across her cheek, down to her chin where he applied a slight amount of pressure to bring her chin up. She wet her dry lips with the tip of her tongue and his gaze riveted on her mouth. "I wouldn't forget kissing a woman as beautiful as you."

"We—we never kissed." Her voice came out wispy, with a catch in the beginning before she got herself under some semblance of control.

"Then I was a fool." His lips were extraordinarily gentle against hers, a mere butterfly's touch.

She could almost convince herself the kiss had not happened; he pulled away so quickly. But the tingling of her lips and excitement churning her insides insisted the kiss was real, no matter how brief.

He took a step back and shoved his hands into the sweatpants pockets. She refused to let her gaze wander downward to where her peripheral vision told her he wasn't entirely unaffected by that quick meeting of their lips.

"A very great fool. Please refresh my memory, for I am at a loss."

"Not such a fool. I was but a young woman. Too young for you, so you said. I was of a different mind." He continued to study her as if he had no idea. So much for her inflated sense of self. He didn't remember her at all. She dipped into a slight curtsey. "Lady Jane Caulfield. I traveled upon your ship from London to the Caribbean. You were less than thrilled to be assigned the duty of keeping a young lady out of harm's way for the duration of the voyage."

His eyes widened and he looked her up and down. She resisted the urge to cross her arms over her chest. Her clothing was modest by today's standards, but with a nineteenth century fashion sense her jeans and scoop-necked blouse were entirely too form fitting for decency.

She should have worn the dress.

"People must age differently in heaven, I suppose, for that was only eight months ago." A sad look came into his eyes. "I wondered what had happened to you. When my travels next brought me to that port, I heard rumors of the Caulfield siblings' disappearance. Runners had been dispatched from London to find you and all were unsuccessful. I hope your death was swift."

She rolled her eyes. He wasn't getting it. "I did not die. Please, believe me. I cast a spell bringing myself and my brother forward in time." She gave a brief history of what had occurred to bring her to this time and place. How a spell of protection surprisingly wrenched a bikini-clad Winnie from the twenty-first century into the nineteenth. How Bastian and Winnie had fallen in love, but a threat to Winnie's life forced Bastian to send her back to the future. Adam knew of Jane and Bastian's escape from London aboard his ship, but he didn't know they'd sought, and found, a spell to bring them forward into Winnie's time.

She glossed over the spell that brought Adam forward, focusing on the fact she had not called him deliberately.

He laughed. "A delightful story. I am greatly entertained." He surveyed the living room. "I should like to learn more of this heaven. Would you be so kind?"

Jane heaved a frustrated sigh and rolled her eyes.

That had gone well.

❄ ❄ ❄

Jane rinsed Adam's salt-water drenched clothing in the sink before sticking them in the dryer. She was at her wits' end. Adam refused to believe he wasn't dead and she wasn't an angel sent to bring him to heaven. How was she to convince him?

Perhaps if they got out of her apartment, the real world would convince him. She tapped her finger on top of the dryer, the vibrations and warmth spreading through her hand. She did need to get him a few things. His clothing wasn't made for winter, and he was clearly uncomfortable in Bastian's too small sweats—as was she, watching the play of muscles so clearly outlined by the ill-fitting items. He'd very nearly caught her staring more than once while they talked.

She'd take him shopping. That alone might convince him he wasn't in heaven. No man of her acquaintance enjoyed picking out clothes. She squinted out the window at the storm outside. They'd have to walk, she wouldn't dare drive in such conditions. Thankfully, there was a shop only a few blocks away. But if the weather got much worse, the store would close and Adam would be out of luck. They better hurry.

The television blasted from the living room at full volume. She ran in to find Adam staring wide-eyed at some movie she didn't recognize. The remote was nowhere to be found. She found the volume control on the side and brought the sound down to a reasonable level, before turning to him, expecting a barrage of questions.

"What is…?" He didn't finish the question. His face turned bright red, his eyes widened even further.

She glanced at the screen to see what had him so

bothered and her own face went up in flames. "Oh, my." She scrambled for the off button, sighing in relief when the screen went black. After all these years, she still had not gotten used to the ease with which nudity was displayed on the television. Awkward didn't begin to describe how the moment felt. She cleared her throat. "That would be the television. Perhaps I can show you how it works a bit later."

He gave her a quick, jerky bow. "That would be fine, thank you." He combed his hair back with his fingers and retied the string that had once again come loose.

The dryer dinged. "Saved by the bell," she murmured to herself. "Your clothing should be dry now," she said in a louder voice so he could hear.

"It has barely been an hour. They couldn't possibly dry in such a short time."

She grinned. Yes, a safe modern invention to discuss. She beckoned him to follow. "Come and see for yourself."

She had him stand right beside her before she pulled the dryer open.

Adam gasped as heat poured over them. He crouched down to look inside and extract his clothes. "So warm, as if they've been hanging in the sun for hours." He put the breeches on top of the washer and reached for the waistband of the sweats.

"What are you doing?" She blocked her eyes with a hand and spun in place so her back was to him. She cursed herself for being reared in the nineteenth century. A modern woman might have been able to enjoy the spectacle of a naked man in her hallway.

"I—I apologize." His voice sounded choked. "I forgot myself."

Lovely. Dry clothes made more of an impression on him than she did. She waved a hand behind her. "Please, think nothing of it. I shall get myself ready and then we will go buy a few things you will have need of here." She scurried down the hall and closed herself into her bedroom, leaned against the door and fanned her flaming cheeks with her hand.

Once she'd calmed her racing pulse, she got ready in moments and they headed to the store.

They plodded their way through the storm to Siddall's Sporting Goods. Surprisingly, they weren't the only ones in the store, but the clerk looked like she was in a hurry to close up.

Jane rushed to find several outfits in Adam's size— underwear and socks, jeans, tee-shirts, sweaters, winter coat, and a sturdy pair of boots.

After trying on the first outfit, Adam came out of the changing room with a frown.

"What's wrong? Do you not like the shirt?" She admired him from head to toe. The cargo-style jeans hung low on his hips and the forest green of the sweater set off his eyes perfectly. She couldn't see a thing wrong.

He held out the price tag attached to the belt loop on the jeans. "I have not the means to pay for these items."

She smiled. "Not to worry. I have plenty of money." She picked up a different sweater. "Why don't you try this next?"

She cast him an inquiring look when he refused to take the clothing from her.

"I believe you now."

She raised her eyebrows in question.

"This is not heaven. I would not be humiliated like this if it were."

"Oh." Understanding dawned. How could she have been so stupid? She should have remembered how proud he was. He hadn't even accepted the money Bastian offered him for keeping an eye on Jane during their voyage, despite the fact he'd been working his hardest to raise money for the tavern he dreamed of owning one day. Not being able to pay his way would be quite a blow for such a man.

She placed a hand on his arm. "It's of no consequence, really. And you need these things. Your own clothing isn't suited for this weather, or this time period. It was my fault you were taken from your time without warning. Please, let me do this for you."

He gave a curt nod. "I have no wish to embarrass you with my appearance. I will find a way to pay back every cent." He whipped around and returned to the dressing room, coming out but a moment later with his old things.

He grabbed all the other items she'd selected and put them all back on their shelves. She gave up and clipped the tags off what he had on, bringing them up to the register.

The cashier gave Adam a raised eyebrow when Jane whipped out her credit card. Jane cringed, hoping Adam hadn't noticed. He stood facing the street, his back ramrod straight, his frown ferocious, and the newly purchased parka zipped tight to his chin.

The store clerk followed them to the door, locking it up tight behind them.

Awkward silence reigned as they hustled along the streets toward her condo. She tried and failed to come up with a topic to smooth over the tension. "Are you all right?" she finally asked.

"I dislike this century. I do not like being dependent on a woman for the clothes on my back or the food on my table." His strides were so long, Jane struggled to keep up. It took him a moment to realize it, but when she fell behind him by a few steps, he slowed his pace and waited for her to catch up. He offered an elbow, which she took, and they proceeded at a much more comfortable pace. "I wish to go back. You can cast your spell upon our return to your home."

It wasn't the blizzard that sent a shard of ice straight through her lungs. She struggled to keep the hurt out of her voice as she responded. "I can't." She quailed at the fury in his gaze. "I mean, I can't do it right now. I need the book, the spell ingredients... It's not something to be done lightly."

"That didn't stop you from bringing me here."

Ouch. That hurt. Mostly because of the truth of it. She hadn't meant to cast the spell, but reciting it at all had been reckless.

Still, since the spell had been to bring forth true love, she'd assumed whomever it conjured would want to be with her. That he would love her. She hadn't even considered that the man might not be happy here, whether he came to love her or not.

He didn't seem to notice the cold, but her cheeks stung and the icy slush seeped through her boots to numb her toes. The wind had picked up since they'd left the store, the snow so thick she had to squint to keep it out of her eyes. With all the cars off the streets, the dim circles of light cast by antique lampposts, and the thick blanket of snow hiding the asphalt road, she almost felt as if she'd been the one transported through time.

Adjusting to the twenty-first century hadn't been all that difficult for her. Of course, she'd had Winnie to smooth her transition. Plus, her status had improved tremendously in this century. The freedoms she'd been denied as a gently bred young lady of the nineteenth century were now a part of her every day life. She supposed it must be completely different for a man. She'd never really discussed that aspect of their travels with Bastian. Nothing was too much for him to handle as long as he had the love of his life, Winnie, at his side.

Adam didn't have a love like that to motivate him. All he had was the nuisance of a girl he'd once been ordered to look after. He didn't have an amazing woman like Winnie.

All he had was her.

❄ ❄ ❄

The following evening, after a day spent bringing Adam up to speed on modern history and inventions, Jane yanked the collar of her wool coat higher against her cheeks to protect them from the frigid December wind. The alley behind The Final Chapter acted like a wind tunnel, sending powder from the roofs swirling about like a whirlwind. The store had remained closed due to the storm, but obviously people had been out and about during the day to trample the deep snow into a slushy mess that seeped right through her boots to freeze her toes. She shivered.

"I rather think we should have waited until morning and simply purchased the book from Susan then. Why must you insist on going home this very instant?" She hid the hurt behind a tone as cold and frosty as the air around them. Once Adam had realized he hadn't died and gone to heaven, he hadn't wasted a moment before deciding he needed to return to his own time immediately.

"I serve no purpose here. And I was this close," He held his finger and thumb a half inch apart. "To purchasing a property to house my tavern. It's a lifetime dream. I simply cannot abandon it now." He fiddled with the lock on the bookstore's back entrance while she scanned the area, waiting for someone to come upon them and condemn them for breaking and entering. Or, at least, for attempting to do so. Adam didn't appear to be having much luck. He'd been at it for the past five minutes with no success.

"I still think this could have waited for a more civilized hour when we could make a legitimate purchase. Simply because Susan wasn't available to open the store for us doesn't give us the right to do as we please. You may find thievery a viable option. I, however, do not." She wrapped her arms around her middle and squeezed. Her stomach had been in knots since the moment he first appeared. The brief joy she'd felt at the idea that he was her true love had faded when she realized he wasn't interested.

"Aha!" With a click, the lock released and the door swung open.

Light from the alley barely penetrated the inky blackness of the bookstore's storage room. Beyond its faint glow, the store was as impenetrable as the pitch black of a ship's hold. She should have thought to bring a flashlight. Finding the spell book wasn't going to be easy in the near dark.

Adam strode inside and was quickly swallowed by the dark. She strained to see into the shadows, but couldn't find him. "Adam?" She hesitated in the doorway.

Tension squeezed the back of her neck. Pain radiated up the base of her skull. The dark hadn't been her friend since she'd gotten stuck in the ship's hold the first week they'd been at sea. Eight years had passed, but she remembered it like it was yesterday. She wiped clammy hands on her thighs and tried to still their shaking.

Adam had been the one to find her. Bastian had practically had to pry her out of Adam's arms. Adam had made her feel so safe, she hadn't wanted to let him go.

Just like that day, he appeared out of the darkness

like an angel sent from heaven just for her. If she weren't so nervous, she might have laughed at how their roles kept reversing.

He took gentle hold of her hand and led her into the store. She glued herself to his side, hugged his arm and followed perfectly along in his footsteps. He glanced down at her and she shivered at the brief flash of heat in his gaze. The look was gone so quickly she could easily believe she'd imagined it. Too soon the utter dark of the store swallowed them and all she could see was his form with no details.

Maybe there was some hope to be had? He'd never looked at her in quite that way when she'd known him last. She'd been too young. He'd seen her as nothing more than a child he had to watch after.

She brought his arm in tighter against her body. If they were successful tonight, she really didn't have the time to be subtle. Or to get him to like her for herself rather than for her body. But if physical attraction could gain her enough time for them to get to know each other better, than she'd use what she had.

"Where's the book?" he whispered.

She averted her face so he wouldn't see her frown. She got her bearings and pointed to their left. "It's about two aisles over. We follow this to the end, make a right and it's two rows over near the endcap."

"Excellent." He didn't appear to have any trouble making his way in the dark.

She stumbled along with him. The only thing keeping her from tripping over unseen obstacles was her grip on his arm.

They reached the correct aisle in no time. Finding the book should have been difficult, but when her hand bumped, painfully, against the little reading table, she felt the leather bound cover against her palm. She'd been so distracted when she realized what she'd done, she'd never put the book back on the shelf.

"Here," she whispered. She kept a firm grip on Adam, and picked up the book with her other hand. A tingle shot up her arm and she almost lost her grip on the heavy book.

"Wonderful. Recite the spell. I've spent enough time here."

"It's not that easy." She just needed a little time. The spell wouldn't have brought him to her if he couldn't love her. Given a little bit of time, maybe he'd come to that realization himself. "Bringing you here was easy. Sending you back can be more difficult. If not done properly, you won't go back to the correct moment. You don't want to go back to the exact moment you left, do you?"

He caught on quickly and shook his head. "No. I'd rather miss the part where I drown. Thank you for your forethought." He bowed deeply before her and she lost her grip on his arm. "Let us return to your home and inspect this carefully so no mistakes are made." He cocked his elbow toward her as gracefully as any lord she'd ever met at a ball.

The ceiling above them squeaked. Jane clutched at Adam's arm. "What was that?"

Adam tilted his head. He pressed a finger to her lips. "Shh."

They stood in silence, listening with all their might. Was it squirrels? The settling of an old building? The soft murmur of a female voice put that thought to rest.

Adam tugged at her arm and they ran to the back door. He peered into the alley, while Jane eased the door shut behind them. With the book clutched in one hand and Adam holding onto her other, she couldn't secure the lock. Light shone from inside the store. Flashlights sweeping back and forth.

Jane shoved at Adam's shoulder and they took off down the alley.

❄ ❄ ❄

Jane rested her head against the back of the couch with a sigh. "I'm sorry, Adam. I don't see how to send you back." They'd been at it for hours. The adrenaline from almost being caught breaking and entering had worn off long since and she could barely keep her eyes open.

He slammed the book onto the coffee table and she jolted up straight. "There must be a way. Find it." He shoved the book toward her. His voice was cold, the look on his face colder. His lips tightened in a thin line, his fists clenched 'til his knuckles were white.

Tears burned her eyes, but she kept them at bay. "I will. This type of magick is difficult, but not impossible. I simply need some assistance. We shall ask my brother to help."

"Is Lord Caulfield a witch as well?"

She winced at the scorn in Adam's voice. The couch suddenly felt hard as a rock under her. She stood and gathered their tea cups. "Naturally. He is quite skilled. I'm sure he'll be able to help me find the way."

"Then we'll go to him now."

Jane nodded. "Let me clean these dishes." As she washed the cups and put them to dry on a hand towel, she glanced out the window. Snow fell thick and heavy outside. She leaned forward to get a glimpse of the street. "We'll have to wait until tomorrow, Adam. This snow is too heavy to venture out in tonight. Walking to the bookstore was one thing, driving out to Bastian's house another. The roads will be closed."

"Nonsense. I'm not worried about a few flakes of snow."

Was he really that eager to get away from her? She gestured out the window. "Take a look for yourself. We're not going anywhere tonight." The snow had picked up again, bringing with it another few inches.

He leaned across the sink to peer out the window. His body brushed up against hers, and she sucked in a breath, then stepped aside to avoid contact.

"I see."

She followed him back to the living room. He picked up the book and opened it to the beginning. The thought of going through those spells one more time made her sick to her stomach.

"I'm exhausted. I am going to retire for the evening. I suggest you do the same."

He stood. "Good evening. I shall see you in the morning." He bowed, sat, and returned his attention to the book, effectively dismissing her.

She swung around and stomped back to her bedroom. She wasn't going to get any sleep.

❄ ❄ ❄

Late the next morning, Jane tiptoed to her bedroom door and pressed her ear against the wood. Nothing. Was he still asleep?

The door opened silently and she slipped out and down the hallway. He lay on her couch, his long legs hung over the arm, his hand flopped off the side to rest on the carpet. The book lay open on his chest, like he'd been reading it when he fell asleep. She should have insisted he retire to her spare room last evening. His neck was twisted at an odd angle as he'd scrunched his body to fit into a space much too small for his huge frame. He would regret sleeping on her sofa.

She crept toward him. "Adam," she whispered.

He didn't respond. She'd let him rest a little longer. Cook him breakfast. Maybe a full stomach would cheer him up after their failure last night.

Eggs, bacon, coffee. Her specialty. Breakfast was the first meal Winnie had taught her to make when they came to this century. She'd never made a meal in her life before her time travel adventure. She'd spent her days painting, singing, and dancing. Working hard to become a properly accomplished lady of the *ton*. Had her father cared anything for her, she would have gone to London to have her season, met a number of eligible gentlemen, and selected a suitable man to marry.

Of course, her father hadn't cared. He'd promised several times, but ultimately must have decided she wasn't worth the expense of a London debut. She suspected he would have picked a husband for her with enough money to enhance her father's coffers rather than a man who would treat his daughter well. She was lucky to have escaped such a fate.

Now she had the opportunity to fall in love with a man of her choosing and marry if, and only if, she so desired. But the only man who'd ever tempted her was asleep on her couch and wished to leave her as soon as humanly possible.

Just her luck.

"My lady?"

She jumped when Adam spoke behind her. How did such a tall man move about so silently? She hadn't realized he'd awoken.

He steadied her by gripping both her elbows. "I apologize for startling you."

She was over her fright but her heart pounded from being so near him. "It's perfectly all right. Did you need something? Breakfast will be ready in a few moments, if you'd like to wash first."

He bowed and headed to the bathroom. She set the table and placed covers over the hot food. Her stomach grumbled from the smell of bacon, so she broke off a piece and popped it into her mouth. Delicious.

"That smells divine. May I join you?"

She swept her arm toward a chair at one end of the small kitchen table. "Please."

He pulled back the chair and looked at her expectantly. When she sat, he pushed her gently into place and took the seat opposite.

They ate in silence a few moments and then Adam cleared his throat. "I must apologize for my behavior last evening. I'm afraid I took my frustration out on you and that was not my intention."

"I understand. This must be difficult for you, dragged out of your own time by a nuisance of a girl you once knew."

He reached across the table and took her hand in his. "You were never a nuisance."

She snorted. "Ha. I overheard you telling the captain you'd never take an assignment like me again." She pulled her hand from his warm grasp and fisted it in her lap. With her other, she pushed cold eggs around the plate with her fork. "I must have been quite a trial for you."

"The opposite."

She gave him a skeptical look. "Really." No, not really. He was being nice. One of the many things she loved about him.

Sincerity shown in the steadiness of his gaze, the soft smile on his lips. "I enjoyed your company much more than I thought proper. You were too young for me, though you always appeared mature beyond your years. And you were the daughter of an earl. I was the third son of a baron with no prospects. A simple sailor who dreamed of one day opening a tavern. I know my place. And it's not as husband to a lady such as you."

"Being the daughter of an earl never brought me any happiness. I would have much preferred to be the wife of a tavern owner."

"If only that were true."

He didn't let her respond. He stood and cleared the table, bringing their dishes to the sink and immediately turning on the water to wash them.

The running water drowned out anything she might have said. Not that it mattered, as she couldn't come up with a single thing to say. What did he mean by that comment? Had he been more interested than she first thought?

"This is truly a wondrous world." He put the last dish on the drying rack and then turned to her. "I watched the box with moving people for quite some time last night as I sifted through the spell book."

"What did you watch?" She wondered what he'd think of some of her favorite shows. Would he even understand what was going on with his limited knowledge of this time?

"Quite a number of different shows. I found one about automobiles particularly interesting. I should very much like to experience this modern mode of transportation."

"Yes. Driving is quite an exhilarating experience. I'm glad you enjoyed yourself last night." Maybe if she got him hooked on a show, she could convince him staying in the future with her was a good idea.

Now she was being ridiculous. Or desperate. It wouldn't take long for her and Bastian to find the key to sending Adam back to his own time. And then he'd be gone from her forever.

Just as she'd known would happen, casting a spell for personal gain would cause her nothing but misery.

She'd found her one true love.

And she was about to lose him.

❄ ❄ ❄

"Don't be ridiculous, Bastian. I am a grown woman. If I choose to entertain a man in my home, or have him live here temporarily or otherwise, I have every right to do so." Jane resisted the urge to throw the telephone against the wall. She'd called her brother for help, not a lecture. She hadn't meant to mention Adam was staying with her, the information had just spilled out when she asked Bastian for help sending Adam home.

"He will leave your home immediately and retire to the Havenport Inn. I'll drive him there myself if he is incapable of navigating the short distance on his own."

Jane rolled her eyes. "Have you looked outside? The roads are impassable. Besides which, he's my guest. I pulled him forward in time, the least I can do is make him comfortable in my home."

"As long as you don't make him too comfortable," Bastian grumbled.

She took a deep breath. One, two, three… "Just what are you implying, brother dear?"

Silence met her on the other end. She could imagine the dismay on his face.

"Jane?" Winnie had taken the phone.

"I believe I may strangle your husband."

Winnie laughed. "No need. I've already done it." Her laughter died down. "You know he only wants what's best for you, right?"

Jane sighed. "I do. And while he would have been well within his rights two hundred years ago, we live in this century now and I quite enjoy the freedoms women are allowed. I refuse to give them up because my brother reverts to a Regency Era lord whenever an issue arises that pertains to me." She flexed her fingers, they'd cramped from being fisted so tight. A deep, calming breath was necessary before speaking again. She didn't want to take her frustrations out on Winnie. "Winnie dear, would you please ask my brother to research this issue? Adam wishes to return home as quickly as possible."

Adam walked into the living room at that moment. She couldn't look at him. He'd made up his mind, she wasn't going to guilt him into staying. She didn't want him like that.

"Of course. He already has your mother's book out. I'm sure he'll find the solution in no time. But." Winnie hesitated. "Are you sure that's what you want? Should we try to delay a bit? If Adam could only have a chance to get to know you, I'm sure he'd never want to leave."

Adam pulled on the new snow boots she'd bought for him yesterday. *Where is he going?*

"Um, can we talk about this later? Now's not a good time."

"Is he there? Can he hear you?"

"Yes."

"Okay. We'll call you when Bastian has something."

"Thank you, Winnie dear."

She hung up and faced Adam. "Are you going somewhere?"

"I shall endeavor to find somewhere else to lay my

head this evening. I have no wish to be the cause of distress for you or your loved ones."

She closed her eyes in exasperation. "You could hear Bastian, I take it."

"It would have been most difficult not to." He gave her a crooked smile and took one of her hands. "I have been remiss not to suggest such a thing myself." His eyes locked on hers, he raised her hand to place a delicate kiss on the backs of her knuckles. "I have no excuse other than to say that my time spent with you has been most enjoyable, and I was loath to leave your presence any sooner than necessary."

She closed the distance between them, trapping their hands against her chest. "Then why leave? Stay. Stay until Christmas at the very least. Give this century a chance. Give *us* a chance to get to know one another. Perhaps you might find you no longer wish to return." She bit her lip. *Please. Please.*

But he shook his head. "Ah, how you tempt me. But tell me. What would I do in this century? How would I support our family?"

Our family. The words rang sweet in her ear. A sharp pang of longing almost made her cry out. Yes. Yes. That's what she wanted. Did he want that too? "You can do whatever you want. I have enough money to support us." The pitch of her voice rose in her excitement. She wrapped her arms around his waist but kept her head tilted back to look him in the eye. Was money the only issue? Such an easy one to solve. "Bastian and I planned well when we left our time. We have enough wealth for anything we wish to do."

Adam gripped her wrists gently to break away from her hug. "Am I to be a kept man, then?"

"I don't see the problem. In our century, it would be said you made an advantageous match."

"It would be said that I married you for your money. Is that how you wish people to see me? As a fortune hunter who took advantage of a beautiful young woman for his own gain?"

Beautiful? A smile pulled at her lips. "Why do you care what others say? We would know the truth. I don't care for the opinions of others."

"And what truth is that? That I love you? That I've been in love with you ever since you first stepped onto my ship eight months, or eight years, ago when we were entirely unsuited? I am as unworthy of you now as I was back then. How would you ever believe that I stayed with you out of love rather than greed?"

"Is that true?" She held her breath. "Did you really fall in love with me back then?"

He closed his eyes, let out a deep breath and opened them again to look straight into hers. "Yes."

Warmth spread from her chest throughout her body. Excitement tingled through her hands as she reached for him. But he moved out of reach.

Her hands dropped back to her sides. "And I love you." Why didn't he sweep her into his arms? "We're meant to be together. How can you let a little thing like money get in the way of that?"

"Money is never a little thing." He ran a hand through his hair, jerking out the tie and tossing it onto the coffee table. He kept his distance, his back straight, a determined expression on his face.

"I can't believe this." Had she really found her true love only to lose him to such nonsense? "You're not even going to give us a chance because I have more money than you?"

"I have nothing, Jane. Nothing to offer you. Everything I owned went down with my ship. My entire life savings. My plans to open a tavern. My skills are worthless here. In time you would come to resent me. I could not bear that."

"That's not true." She dashed tears off her cheek with the back of her hand. "I wouldn't have believed you to be such a coward."

He stiffened. His frown deepened, lines etched deep into his forehead. A muscle ticked in his jaw.

"You're afraid to take a chance on me and you're making up this ridiculous excuse. Well, fine." She grabbed her pink parka and her purse, then stomped to the door. "I'll make it easier on you. When the phone rings, answer it. It will be Bastian calling with a spell to send you home. I'm going out."

She yanked the door open and stepped out into the frigid afternoon air. The wind hit her square in the face, but she ignored it. She zipped her jacket all the way up, put her chin down, and walked away.

❄ ❄ ❄

Jane trudged down the snow covered Main Street sidewalk. The plows had been out. Despite what she'd said to Bastian, the roads had been cleared fairly well. Only the side streets remained relatively untouched. She made her way to Mellie's Diner, which was, blessedly, open.

She draped her parka over an empty stool at the counter and dropped onto the red, glittery vinyl seat next to it. Mellie had once told Jane she'd modeled her diner after a fountain shop she'd loved when she was a teenager in the '50s. The tourists definitely seemed to like it. Mellie's had a thriving business during the season.

Jane ordered their celebrated cinnamon latte. She wrapped her hands around the oversized mug and let the warmth seep into her fingers.

She wasn't going to cry. She refused. The burning sensation in her eyes was from the cold, not tears.

"Ms. Caulfield?"

Jane looked up to see the mother of one of her students standing over her. "Mrs. Li. So nice to see you. How is Ravenne enjoying her holiday?"

"She's doing well, thank you." Mrs. Li sat next to her, leaning one elbow on the counter. "I hope you don't mind my asking, but, are you okay?"

Jane wiped her nose with her napkin. "I'm fine, thank you. Nothing to worry about."

Mrs. Li smiled, but looked unconvinced. "Are you waiting for your boyfriend?"

"Boyfriend?" Jane's voice squeaked at the end. How could anyone know about Adam already? He'd been here all of three days and most of that time they'd been stuck inside due to the snow.

"My husband was at Siddall's yesterday—our power was flickering so he went to purchase a lantern. He saw you and your friend. He thought you were paying for the man's clothing. I said, 'Nonsense. Ms. Caulfield is a sensible woman. She can do much better than a man who can't afford his own clothing.' I would hate to think of someone taking advantage of you in such a manner." Mrs. Li's face was alive with interest; her eyes bright, her head cocked to the side. She nodded her head and watched Jane expectantly.

Maybe Adam had a point. Not about her resenting him. That was plain stupid. But he had a great deal of pride. How would he feel if everywhere he went, people glared at him for taking advantage of poor little Ms. Caulfield, the elementary art teacher? He'd hate it.

And so would she. She'd probably give them all a piece of her mind, which would likely jeopardize her position at the school. She didn't need to work, but she loved teaching art to her young students. She didn't want to give that up any more than she wanted to give up Adam.

"Ms. Caulfield?"

"Oh, I'm sorry, Mrs. Li. I'm afraid I have a bit of a cold." Jane faked a sneeze into her napkin and resisted smiling when Mrs. Li leaned way back on her stool. "I really shouldn't have ventured out, but I was hoping a nice latte would make me feel better."

"Do take care of yourself. You wouldn't want to spread those nasty germs to any of your students when school resumes in the new year."

"Definitely not. I'll see you soon. Enjoy the rest of winter break." Jane whipped her jacket on and raced out of the diner. There had to be a way around the problem of money, or Adam's lack thereof. But if they only had a short time together, she wasn't going to waste it sulking.

❄ ❄ ❄

Jane cautiously entered her condo and removed her jacket, hanging it on the coat tree near the front door. "Adam?"

He appeared at the kitchen door. "Jane." He crossed his arms over his chest and frowned at her. "I'm pleased to see you are well." He didn't *look* happy to see her. "By the time I was able to lace up these damn boots, I was unable to find your tracks. No fewer than three couples and their children chose this afternoon to play in the snow directly outside."

"I'm sorry. I didn't mean to worry you."

He nodded. "I apologize for my words earlier. I would not hurt you for the world and yet that appears to be all I am capable of doing."

She gathered her courage, walked right up to him, and stood on her tip-toes to give him a kiss. She meant to be brief, but the feel of his lips on hers was intoxicating and she lingered longer than was proper. When she finally came to her senses, she found herself held tightly in his embrace, her breathing ragged and uneven.

He ran his hand through her hair, then cupped the base of her skull gently. "Ah, you don't know what you do to me. I lose all reason in your presence."

"I'm sick of reason. I don't want to think. I don't want to talk about the future or worry about the past. If all we have is the time it takes Bastian to come up with a spell to send you back, then I don't want to spend that time worrying or avoiding you. I want to be with you. I want to enjoy the time we have, no matter how short."

"I have no wish to make this harder on either of us."

She nodded. "I know. It's going to be awful. But I understand why you can't stay. You need to have a life outside of me to be happy. And I can't give that to you. You simply don't belong here. Just as I no longer belong back then." She blinked back tears. "You're right. Eventually, we'd grow to resent each other. I would rather end this now, than have that happen." She grabbed his hand and pulled him toward the couch. "So, I'll take what time we have and savor the memories when you're gone."

He stood his ground until she stopped tugging on his hand. "Are you sure?" he asked.

"I'm sure."

That was a lie. She wasn't sure at all.

❄ ❄ ❄

Jane folded the last corner of the wrapping paper and secured it with a small piece of tape. The bright green and gold paper was festive yet elegant. She wrapped a gold satin ribbon around it and tied a pretty bow. They'd agreed not to exchange presents this morning, but wait until the whole family was together. She had no idea what Adam could have gotten her without a penny to his name.

She had to stop fussing. If they didn't leave for Bastian and Winnie's in the next five minutes, they'd be late for Christmas dinner. And Adam wouldn't care about the wrapping anyway. The contents were what were really important.

The problem was she didn't actually want to give the present to him. The book was appropriate, yes. And something he would most definitely appreciate. But the thought of him using the spell she'd written based on the contents of the book and Bastian's suggestions had her stomach knotted in pain.

The spell would work. She knew it. And when Adam said the words, she'd never see him again.

The last few days had been magical. While Bastian studied ways to improve her spell, she and Adam had spent all their time together. She'd shown him all her favorite spots in town and he'd told her all about his plans for his tavern. They'd tried to pack away as many memories of each other as possible in the short time they had left.

She'd almost hung up on Bastian last night when he called to tell her he'd figured out the last piece to complete the spell. But she'd promised Adam and she wasn't going to let him down, no matter how much she hurt.

Adam was on the phone when she finally emerged. He was a quick study and had picked up on how to use modern technology with relative ease.

The huge pile of presents she'd put aside for the girls was gone. He must have packed them in her SUV while she was wrapping his gift.

His eyes glowed with appreciation as he watched her. He said goodbye to whomever was on the phone and placed the receiver in its cradle on the end table. "You look absolutely stunning."

She glanced down at her form-fitting black slacks and red sweater. She'd chosen her outfit with care. Modest, yet attractive. She was going to her brother's house after all. She couldn't wear the silk dress with the slit halfway up her thigh she'd driven Adam wild with last night or one of the low cut blouses and hip hugger jeans he seemed to like so much on her.

"You look amazing as well." He'd finally consented to having her purchase an appropriate outfit for this dinner, though he'd insisted she take the only item of value he had on him—an antique chain and watch that had somehow managed to stay in his pocket through his near drowning. She'd found it yesterday on the laundry room floor where it must have fallen from his pocket. Khaki pants clung to his muscular thighs and hugged his butt in just the right way. He'd left his dark green button down shirt open at the collar. The color made the green in his hazel eyes pop. He looked gorgeous. "Who was that on the phone?"

"Winnie."

"What did she want?" They would be there soon enough. What couldn't wait a few minutes?

"I had asked her to look into something for me."

She raised her eyebrows inquiringly. "Oh? What?"

He waved off her question. "We can discuss it later.

We better get going or we shall be late."

Jane was dying to ask more questions, but Adam remained silent during the fifteen minute drive to Bastian and Winnie's home on the outskirts of town.

Chaos reigned once they arrived. Wrapping paper and empty boxes surrounded the twelve foot tree decorated with tiny white lights, glass balls, and homemade ornaments. New toys littered the floor.

"Auntie Jane, Auntie Jane!" Rose and Holly called out when Jane pushed open the door, not bothering to ring the bell.

The girls got right to the heart of the matter and pounced on the presents Adam carried. Over the course of the next few hours, they monopolized Jane so she had no time to get Adam or Winnie alone, though the two of them spent a great deal of time talking and staring intently at Winnie's computer.

When the girls were finally tucked tight in their beds after stories not only from their parents but from Auntie Jane and their new friend Adam as well, it was time for the adults to exchange gifts.

Two bottles of wine were consumed as they laughed and exclaimed their delight at their gifts. Christmas carols played softly in the background.

Jane took a fortifying sip of her drink when it was time to present her gift to Adam. She handed him the package and sat back, legs crossed, arms wrapped protectively around herself.

He unwrapped the book slowly, as if he didn't particularly want it either. He played with the bookmark inserted into the correct page, but didn't open the book to read what was inside.

"The spell is complete. There's an envelope inside with all the ingredients you need. Whenever you're ready…" She couldn't complete the sentence.

She needed air. The fire blazing in the hearth that had seemed so comforting and beautiful before, now sucked all the air out of the room. She swept her tongue around her mouth to ease the dryness and tasted the salt of sweat beading on her upper lip.

"If you'll excuse me." She leaped up and practically flew to the bathroom. When would he cast the spell? Would he do it right away? Would he at least spend the night? Wait until after New Years?

A knock sounded on the door. "Jane?" Winnie called. "Are you all right?"

"I'm fine. I just need a minute." *Liar*. She was anything but fine.

❄ ❄ ❄

Jane took at least ten minutes to get herself under control. She'd known this moment was coming. She had to face it.

Bastian and Winnie were alone in the living room when she finally came out. She quickly ducked back into the hall. They were locked in a heated embrace on the sofa next to the tree.

Where was Adam? She searched the kitchen and dining room, but didn't spot him. She strode across the foyer to check the den. Her heart dropped when she saw the front door was ajar.

No. He wouldn't. Would he?

He'd left her. So eager to get away from her, he hadn't bothered to say goodbye first.

And she'd believed him when he said he loved her.

Fool.

No. She wouldn't allow it. He had every right to

return from whence he came, but that didn't give him the right to leave without so much as a friendly wave goodbye.

She yanked on the snow boots she'd left by the door. Not wanting to waste time heading into the guest room for her coat, she wrenched the door open wide and ran out onto the front porch.

Christmas lights glistened on the porch rails and the neighbors' homes. The road had been cleared, but snow piled up on either side, making it difficult to see down the street.

The world appeared peaceful—in direct contrast to the turmoil spreading through her chest.

She looked about wildly, trying to figure out which direction Adam had taken. A lone figure stood at the far end of the driveway. Adam.

She marched up to him. His back was to her, so she punched him on the shoulder to get his attention. He swung around, rubbing his shoulder. Surprise colored his expression. Raised eyebrows, a crooked grin.

She was going to miss that grin. "You can't even bother to say goodbye? The girls will be in tears when they realize you've left without telling them." The girls weren't the only ones.

"The girls? What about you?" He crossed his arms over his chest. "Would you shed a tear or wish me good riddance?"

She wrapped her arms around her midsection. The wind slipped through her knit sweater as if she were naked.

Adam whipped off his coat and swung it around her shoulders, stepping in close to do so.

She closed her eyes and inhaled deeply as the warmth of his jacket surrounded her. Her last chance to memorize his scent. Memories would be all she had of him.

He didn't step back so she tilted her head to look up at him. "My feelings are entirely beside the point."

He ran a finger down her cheek. "I beg to differ. I believe your feelings are of the utmost importance at this moment." He kissed the tip of her nose. "Tell me, Jane. Do you wish me to stay?"

"I will not stand in your way. Coming here was not of your choosing. I understand your wish to return to where you were happy."

"Then why did you come rushing out here? Why did you punch me in the arm in such a manner?"

Heat flooded her frozen cheeks. "I was merely trying to gain your attention. I apologize."

Adam slipped one arm around her waist and drew her close. She kept her gaze somewhere in the vicinity of his neck. Confusion muddled her thoughts. What did he mean by this? What did he want her to say?

"I don't think that's it," he whispered in her ear. "I think you'd miss me terribly. I think you're dying to ask me to stay here—with you. Because you love me."

She gasped. How could he be so cruel? "Of course I want you to stay. I've made no secret of that fact. You're the one who insists you must go back."

"And now you've given me the means to go. Because you want me to be happy even if it makes you miserable." He gently, but insistently, put pressure on her chin and forced her to look into his eyes. Then he brushed his lips against hers in a whisper of a kiss. "Because you love me. Almost as much as I love you."

She threw her arms around his neck. "I do. I love you." She buried her face against his chest. "Please stay," she mumbled. "I don't care if I have to take care of you until we're old and gray. I could never resent you. I love you."

"I would hate myself. But that's not going to happen

because with a little help from your brother, I've discovered a way to make my own way in this century."

She pulled back to stare at him wide-eyed. "What? How?"

"It occurred to me that I know exactly where a nineteenth century merchant ship with valuable cargo was lost at sea. Lady Caulfield conducted a search on that amazing machine—a computer, I believe she called it?—and discovered the ship was never found. With the promise of a percentage of the profit, Bastian has agreed to hire a salvage company to search for *The Sea Witch*. Should we be successful, I shall have sufficient funds to open my tavern. If not, then I shall find another way." He tucked a lock of her hair behind her ear and rested his forehead against hers. "I will build something of which we can both be proud. Something to pass down to our children."

Jane couldn't believe what she was hearing. "Do you mean you aren't going back? You're going to stay with me?"

"I wouldn't leave you for the world."

The soft words of *Baby, It's Cold Outside* drifted through the open door.

"The song speaks the truth." Adam lifted her into his arms. "But I know just how to warm you up," he said with a wicked grin. "And I'm not going anywhere."

Curious about Jane's first run-in with magick? Find out how she cast a spell to protect her brother Bastian Caulfield, and ended up bringing twenty-first century romance author, Winnie Boyle, from the beaches of Star Island to a country estate in Regency England.

IN HER DREAMS is available in the anthology— TIMELESS ESCAPES: A Collection of Summer Stories.

About the Author

EMMA KAYE is married to her high school sweetheart and has two beautiful kids that she spends an insane amount of time driving around central New Jersey. Before ballet classes and tennis entered her life, she decided to try writing one of those romances she loved to read and discovered a new passion. She has been writing ever since. Add in a playful puppy and an extremely patient cat and she's living her own happily ever after while making her characters work hard to reach theirs.

❄ ❄ ❄

For more information on Emma, please visit her online at www.emma-kaye.com, on Facebook at www.facebook.com/emmakayewrites, on Twitter at www.twitter.com/emmakayewrites or on GoodReads at www.goodreads.com/emma-kaye.

Also by Emma Kaye

Love time travel?
Try another Emma Kaye time travel romance.

❄ ❄ ❄

Time for Love

A woman finds much more than she bargained for when she travels through time to Regency England.

Echoes of the Past

Can a time traveling witch find love in present day Lobster Cove, Maine, or will her curse get in the way?

For You

A time traveler and an earl's widow find love in Regency London—but time may not be on their side.

❄ ❄ ❄

<u>Timeless Tales – Short Stories</u>

Granting Her Wish featured in Timeless Keepsakes

In Her Dreams featured in Timeless Escapes

Losing Patience featured in Timeless Treasures

To Have and to Hold featured in Timeless Vows

<u>Havenport – Novellas</u>

Under Her Spell featured in Welcome to Havenport

The Ghost of You featured in Haunted Havenport

Snowbound in Havenport — Fall, 2017

White Christmas

Nicole S. Patrick

❄ ❄ ❄

Prosecutor Savannah Moore's life changed in an instant. Career on hiatus, recovering from an attack, she finds solace for the holidays in the town of Havenport, Rhode Island. A change of pace for sure. Just what she needs to heal and rebuild her confidence to testify against her attacker. An unexpected meeting of gorgeous Marc "Mac" MacDonald leaves Savannah unsure of her next move. Should she stay in Havenport with this brave, sexy, and hard, yet gentle former Marine? Or, should she return to the crazy life of courtrooms and cases? Mac helps her understand that taking one day at a time might lead to a future she least expected.

Mac MacDonald has finally found a place to call home. A place where he feels part of a family. His car repair business is booming, his former girlfriend and all her drama is history, and he's ready to move on to the next chapter in his life. Savannah Moore is cute, sexy, and tougher than she looks. But when someone tries to hurt her, Mac realizes he's never had this intense degree of protective instincts for anyone, not even in combat. Savannah has touched a place in his heart that surprises and thrills him. Can he convince her to let this thing between them grow?

❄ ❄ ❄

Dedicated to ~

Pop. The best father-in-law I could ever have wished for.
Miss you.

White Christmas
by Nicole S. Patrick

"Brutus, come back here!" Savannah yanked the leash as gently as possible to avoid strangling the Scottie. "Ugh." He was strong for a little thing. Must be trying to channel an Alaskan Husky in the Iditarod.

Brutus was also a devil camouflaged in a cute, white, fluffy package. Talk about a wolf in sheep's clothing. But his owner was one of her sister's best customers at Wags and Walks, so Savannah kept her opinions to herself.

The weather was unseasonably warm for a December morning or, perhaps Havenport only felt that way since she was used to the brutal wind and cold of Chicago. A tolerable ocean breeze floated over the quaint town, but the weatherman on *Rhode Island Today* reported they were in for a wallop of a snowstorm. With the holidays a little more than a week away, a white Christmas might just happen.

Savannah steered Brutus around a snow pile and he

stopped to sniff something nonexistent while she unzipped her puffy Northface jacket. With the leash between her teeth, she shrugged out of the sleeves then tied the jacket around her waist with a swift tug. Brutus, the monster, found her struggle fascinating, for he stared up at her with an amused look on his hairy snout.

She took the leash out of her mouth and smirked. "Ha! I didn't lose a grip on you this time, mister." His short bark made her grin. Brutus was lovable when he wasn't terrorizing other dogs. Last week he'd bullied Mrs. Pruitt's Chihuahua, Taco, in the park. The jury was still out on who'd won that round. Taco was a tough little guy, too.

Large evergreen wreaths and alternating shiny silver bells hung from the antique lampposts lining the street. The row of shops' windows decorated for the Christmas season. For the first time in a long time she looked forward to the holidays—baking cookies, wrapping presents, and spending it with Augusta.

Moving here last month had been…well…a change. A change she still wasn't sure would be long-term. Nonetheless, Augusta was thrilled. For far too long, work had made visiting her sister on a regular basis impossible.

Not anymore. Things had changed in an instant— her career on hiatus and the future uncertain. Sometimes thinking about it made the stress level in her head explode.

"One day at a time," she mumbled, and Brutus whined in agreement as he sniffed the hydrant and did a potty trot around the area. According to his neurotic owner, Brutus was pee shy. She let out the retractable leash and turned away as he prepared to do his business.

A sign in the window of the bookstore The Final Chapter caught her eye. Romance author book signing. Her favorite romance author, Winnie Boyle, and a few other authors were scheduled to visit in a few days. Awesome. Winnie's books were her guilty pleasure and had gotten her through many all-nighters in law school.

The store was adorable. The window housed a beautifully decorated tree, along with a hodgepodge of books and various knickknacks. Savannah pressed her nose against the glass and peered at the cover of Winnie's latest paperback. *Holy hotness.* That cover model was to die for, with muscles on top of muscles. That kind of man only existed on book covers, not in this sleepy town.

But, to meet a guy resembling that delicious cover model would be—

A short bark followed by a familiar growl penetrated her drool fest and the leash cut into her palm. *Uh oh.*

"Whoa, what the…" a deep voice shouted from the vicinity of the closest parked car. There was no one in sight, including Brutus. His leash stretched to its limit.

"You better not have bitten anyone mister," she muttered, thinking of a few-hundred ways to make his little doggy life miserable if he had. Walking him was worse than babysitting a child. Brutus sauntered into view with a shit-eating grin on his doggy face and his tail wagging high and fast. The person on the other end of that deep voice popped up from behind the parked car— a tire iron in one hand and a soaking wet shirtfront.

Her mouth dropped open. His flannel stretched quite nicely over an impressive set of pectorals, and for a nanosecond Savannah imagined *him* on the cover of a romance novel.

The forest green of his shirt turned almost black from the spreading stain.

"Your dog peed on me." His lips clamped into a thin line and he pushed a lock of his long, dark hair away from his forehead.

Yep—definitely cover model material. Bet he'd be

great dressed as a pirate, or a duke maybe.

Later she'd probably think back on this moment and kick herself for the lack of an appropriate comeback—something snappy, or snarky, or even polite. But at seven fifteen a.m., all she could think to do was giggle and bite her lip to keep from laughing.

"You find this amusing?" He tilted his head and his dark eyebrows winged into a vee.

He was sunburned, which was unusual for December. Maybe he worked outdoors, or maybe it was windburn. And that's when she noticed a white line on the left side from temple to cheek—the long pucker of a scar. Staring was rude—so Gran always said—but she couldn't tamp down her natural curiosity, especially when it had to do with scars.

"Um…no…of course I don't." She shook her head—quite vigorously. Maybe it would knock some sense into her and squash the giggles bubbling.

He didn't seem to believe her if his glare was any indication. Whatever had caused the injury didn't detract from his amazing eyes—hazel with flecks the color of caramel.

At the thought of caramel, her stomach growled, reminding her she hadn't eaten breakfast. The image of a double latte with extra whipped cream and a scone from Led Zeppoli bakery popped in her head.

The man moved around the front bumper and Brutus, sensing oncoming conflict, growled.

"Call off your junior attack dog, or I'll pee on *him*," he said between gritted teeth.

She blinked. "That's illegal."

One eyebrow arched.

"Peeing in public," she added quickly. "You'll get a summons at the very least. Well, the first offense is $250, then it's more." She clamped her mouth shut at his scowl.

Why not just site case precedents to him while you're at it? Old habits died hard.

Brutus—thank his cranky little soul—decided to stand in front of her and bare his doggy teeth.

The man shrugged. "Back off, you little devil. I'm not going to do anything but send your owner here my dry cleaning bill."

"Oh I'm not his owner," she stated, pointing to the logo on her shirt, which covered her left boob. *Good going, pointing out the boobage.* "Funny, I think he's a demon most days too." She smiled and patted Brutus' head.

No comment.

Savannah blew out a breath. *Okay, so much for trying to defuse the situation with small talk.* "I'm really sorry about your shirt." She stifled a dreaded chuckle. She couldn't seem to control them. What in the world was wrong with her this morning? "I'll pay for it."

Clearly the man did not appreciate her mirth. Jeez, it wasn't as if Brutus had done number two on his boots. Plus, with the grease on his jeans, he obviously didn't have a problem getting dirty. His phone rang, thankfully breaking their awkward moment. He reached into his pocket, and frowned at the screen.

"Oh, you'll pay for it," he warned before he answered the call, and she *thought* there was a slight tilt to the corner of his mouth, but it was gone in a second. He turned away and engaged in his conversation, leaving her to stare at his back.

He had a nice back, and broad shoulders, and...*nope*, she would not check out what was under his Levis, as much as she wanted to.

Time to go.

She whistled for Brutus and tugged on his leash. Should she hand the man the card for the store, so he knew where to send that bill? Not that she *wanted* to see him and his grumpy self again. Oh well, Havenport was small enough. They'd likely cross paths.

Savannah wasn't sure if that was a good or a bad thing.

"And how was my best boy? Did you behave?" Savannah's lunch lodged in her throat at April Welch's— Brutus' neurotic owner—whining baby-talk voice.

A vision of Cruella de Vil's younger sister came to mind. April's spotted fur coat and matching boots were a bit much. Savannah knew it irked Augusta's animal activist beliefs when anyone wore fur.

"Well, actually he…" she began, ready to tell April about Brutus and his pee adventure.

"Was wonderful as usual." Augusta cut her off with a glare, and scurried to hand over his leash and gold plated water bowl, then ushered them out. April's fake laugh trilled as the door closed.

Savannah finished sorting the shipment of combs and grooming brushes for display before regarding her sister. "Why not tell her the truth? April needs to know her *best boy* is terrorizing your other clients."

Augusta leaned against the glass counter and sighed so heavy her bangs shifted. "Because she's my best customer. And, believe it or not, I do need to eat."

Since opening the shop a little more than a year prior, Augusta had busted her butt to drum up business. The locals—many of whom made their homes seasonally in Havenport—handed over their dogs or hired a puppy sitter while they shopped or sailed, or whatever rich people did during the day. Besides herself and Jacob, the high school kid who occasionally showed up, she and Augusta were it as far as employees went.

"You need to advertise more. Tonight I'll research

how to make your social media accounts work better." An evening staying in with a pint of Rocky Road sounded heavenly. It wasn't as if she had anything else to do on a Friday night.

"And *you* need to get out and meet people, instead of hibernating with your computer and ice cream."

Meeting Peed-On Guy *technically* counted, but Savannah wasn't about to bring it up again. Augusta didn't know who he was, based on her description, and it wasn't as if they'd exchanged names. He probably didn't live in Havenport. "Not interested," she replied, although for some unexplained reason disappointment stuck in her throat at the thought of never seeing him again.

Augusta shook her head in disgust. "Yeah, yeah, I know. I won't push it. Speaking of advertising, I forgot to tell you about my idea." Her expression lighted as bright as the battery operated Christmas wreath hanging on the front door.

Uh oh. Here comes another one of her brilliant endeavors. Augusta was definitely a glass is half-full person. She oozed with overflowing enthusiasm every day. Whereas *she*, on the other hand, was more logical and practical, which *had* made her a damned good lawyer.

"Idea?" The question escaped before she could help herself.

Augusta beamed. "It's going to be great."

Savannah resisted the urge to snort. Augusta had uttered those words many times before and the outcome was never *great*.

"Local dog owners are coming here tomorrow for a photo shoot for a calendar I'm creating," Augusta explained. "I'll need you to set up the props."

Savannah stopped midway of hanging the items on display. "What props?"

"Jacob's drama teacher lent us backdrops and all

kinds of stuff. He delivered them to the back room while you were out." Augusta flitted around the store like a butterfly. It was exhausting to watch. "All proceeds will go to the animal shelter, but with the Wags and Walks name on top, I'm hoping to bring in new customers."

The concept had promise. "How are you going to pay for printing, and who's doing the layout?" Fine details weren't exactly Augusta's strong suit.

Augusta bit her lip and gave her a sly grin. "Well…you know so much more about computers than I do, Savvy."

Not surprising. Augusta roped her into things all the time. Ever since they were in school and Augusta "borrowed" her term papers to call her own—it was the ongoing saga of big sister coming to little sister's rescue.

Until Augusta had turned into *her* rock just when she'd needed it most. For that Savannah was eternally grateful.

The events leading up to her move to Havenport surfaced, but she shut them down right away. No use getting maudlin or Augusta would never let up about her getting out more.

"Fine, I'll help." The calendar idea *had* merit, especially from a charity angle, and it might be an excellent way to drum up business. "But this better not come back to bite me, no pun intended." For some reason she knew it would turn into a fiasco. Savannah remembered Augusta's foray into rescuing rabbits when they were kids. Memories of bunny poop in her shoes and the chewed pages of her textbooks made her shudder.

Augusta grinned. "I knew I could count on you."

"I am not taking the pictures," she warned.

"Oh don't worry about that." Augusta waved a hand. "Pete at the newspaper is doing the photos and printing for free. I think he likes me." She shrugged while refilling water and food bowls for clients coming in later this afternoon.

Of course Pete liked Augusta—who didn't? She was tall, curvy, and the most bubbly person in the world. Augusta's midnight hair reached her butt and she had a natural exotic beauty that caused double takes by most men.

She, on the other hand, had gotten the short Moore genes from the English-Scottish side of the family. She rarely tanned and blushed easily. Sure, the blonde hair— thanks to the salon—enhanced her baby blues, which many told her were her best feature, but nothing could be done for her lack of cleavage. Nothing natural that is.

Oh well, at least she could eat anything and not gain weight—hence the pints of Rocky Road stacked in her freezer. "What time is this happening, and how many are you expecting?"

She straightened a pile of dog magazines in the rack and spotted Brutus' extra doggy sweater hanging on a peg by the door. "Wait, is April involved?"

Augusta pretended to ignore the question, which was answer enough.

"You better hope Brutus behaves."

"Twelve models are coming with their dogs—one for each month of the year." Augusta ignored the Brutus comment too. "There are props for every season, and a snow making machine, which I have no idea how to use. Could you figure it out?" Augusta implored.

She growled. "All right. I'll take a look at it."

"Love you," Augusta's voice rang out as Savannah made her way to the back room.

Dogs and snow making machines were a far cry from courtrooms and juries.

❄ ❄ ❄

"Mac, phone call for you in the office." Carol's voice piped through the intercom.

"Can you take a message? I'm almost done here," he called out above the Stones tune blasting from the speaker system he'd installed in the garage. One more tightening should do it. He placed the socket wrench on the bench and sopped his sweaty brow with his shirtsleeve.

Carol cracked open the door from the reception area and peeked in. "It's that nice Augusta who owns the pet shop, confirming you and Sniper for this afternoon."

"Huh?"

Carol *tsked*. "I reminded you yesterday morning." At his shrug she continued. "The photos of you and Sniper for the calendar to raise funds for the animal shelter?"

He racked his brain but only came up with the memory of getting pissed on yesterday morning by that grumpy terrier. Too bad the pretty blonde walking the mutt had hightailed it by the time he'd finished arguing with Gena. His ex had a knack for screwing with his concentration, and by the time he'd thought to look up the blonde, the day was over.

The logo on her shirt popped into his mind, along with that adorable blush when she pointed it out to him.

"Wags and Walks, right?" He wasn't thrilled the runt had ruined his favorite shirt, but the dog's handler had piqued his curiosity. She was cute in a petite and athletic way. "When do I have to be there?"

"Two. So you have plenty of time to go home and clean up." She wrinkled her nose.

He sent her a lopsided grin. "Yes, *Mom*."

"Someone's got to keep you in line." Carol winked.

"Oh, and don't forget Christmas dinner next week is at my house," she said and closed the door.

Upon hiring Carol to run the office for his car repair shop, he had no idea she'd turn into his surrogate mother. But he liked the attention—not to mention Carol's weekly care packages. There was enough meatloaf in his freezer for the next month. It was going to be nice to spend the holiday with a family for a change.

Mac put the tools back in their rightful places, vaguely remembering Augusta telling him about the calendar. He'd met her a few times at the shelter when he stopped in to donate food. Since he'd adopted Sniper from the animal shelter, it was only right to give back. From the moment all one hundred pounds of English Mastiff puppy had pounced on him, their bond formed.

Keeping up with the amount of food the dog consumed was another story. Big boy was pushing one seventy, and it was high time he went on a diet and exercise regimen. Business had picked up considerably lately—not that he was complaining—but that left less time for Sniper.

Maybe he'd hire Wags and Walks.

Mac cleaned up at the slop sink and wiped down his tools. Keeping his repair shop in pristine condition was hard work, but his clients with their high-end cars did not appreciate dirt and grime on their luxury seats.

He grimaced at the mirror. Carol was right. Sweat and grease streaks ran down his cheeks and over his sunburn. His nose hurt like hell. He'd forgotten how strong the sun was on the west coast even in December.

Los Angeles, his condo on the beach, and, thankfully, Gena were history. The trip out there last week was his last. Maybe he should feel bad that Gena had accused him of wasting three years of her precious life on an "unemotional, cold-hearted bastard" but oddly, he didn't. She'd wanted commitment. Hell, her idea of commitment was him making all the money and her spending all of it. The plan had been to settle down and build his high-end repair business and what better place than LA, with its celebrities and rich people. That hadn't panned out.

Crap, the sunburn made the scar on his cheek stand out like a white streak of lightning. "Now that's going to look ridiculous on the calendar," he muttered. Nothing he could do now, and it wasn't as if he were ashamed of it.

He'd served his country, was a Marine through and through, and damned proud of it. Something else Gena could never understand. His Corps brothers were important, and whenever one needed a little help after a deployment, he was more than happy to give him a place to hang his hat. Coming home from war, re-acclimating to civilian life—hell, that was tough. He remembered his first days back in the States. And for some guys, their families weren't supportive. At all.

"Ah, so much for that chapter in the MacDonald story." All the Gena drama was over.

MCD Repairs was growing and he couldn't be happier, but a little female companionship might be nice, too. Maybe he'd get to see that blonde again. A hint of anticipation crept into his gut at the thought.

He tossed the rags in the laundry bin and glanced at the antique car clock on the wall. A few minutes before noon—time enough to hit the head, get showered, and back to town.

Wags and Walks was chaos central. Barking dogs, squeaking chew toys, a snow machine spitting out burnt smelling Styrofoam. Where was a pint of Rocky Road when she needed it?

"Savvy, we're done with June. Can you get the American flag stuff for July?" Augusta asked.

So much for squeezing in bites of her soggy PB&J sandwich between May's poodle and June's Jack Russell terrier.

"Sure." She hopped off the stool from behind the register and headed to the back room. Where was the damned Uncle Sam hat? When she'd organized the stuff last night, everything had been in its rightful place—now, it looked like disaster struck. There it was, on the bottom shelf behind the blowup palm tree and a giant pumpkin.

Crouching, she squeezed between the two shelving units. Thank God her top half was small. Augusta couldn't have fit. "God, it's dusty." She coughed, and held in a sneeze. Was that a spider? "Eww…" *One…more…inch.* "Got it!"

"Ouch." Unscrewing her body from between the shelves wasn't easy. Finally free, she sucked in dust-free air and…"Yuck!" Doggy drool hit the side of her nose, along with the sharp smell of beef jerky. A deep *woof* invaded the small space and a giant head came into focus. *Holy!* The head pushed forward and she fell—hard—right on her ass.

She stared up at the gargantuan dog and prayed for a quick death. She'd survived the knife attack, and surgeries, and wouldn't this be the icing on the cake to be eaten by a slobbering beast. *Lovely.* Paws landed on either side of her legs. *It*—she couldn't tell if the thing was male or female—proceeded to lick her cheeks, and nose, and earlobe.

"Stop that." She swatted at the wet snout and covered her head with both arms.

"Sniper! Heel!" The sharp command cut through the air and the slobber ceased.

Savannah peeked through her crossed arms and her

heart nearly stopped. *Of all people.* Peed-On Man stood above her, arms crossed, much taller and bigger than she'd remembered from yesterday.

Payback was a bitch.

The corner of his mouth lifted. "You need help?" He stuck out a hand, but she eyeballed his dog. "He won't move."

Glad *he* was so sure. She swallowed hard and reached up.

Calloused and large, his warm hand engulfed hers and a jolt of electricity tingled into her palm. The amusement in his eyes sent that jolt straight down to her toes. In one swift motion, he hauled her to her feet causing her to suck in a swift breath. Involuntarily, she rubbed her shoulder. Damn. She usually avoided sudden moves with her bad arm.

"Are you okay?" He sounded concerned and hadn't released her hand.

"Yeah, fine. Um…thanks." Guess feeling like a wet rag had affected her brain. Her lack of formulating a single coherent thought had absolutely nothing to do with the beautiful man *still* holding her hand.

Nope. Not a thing.

She pulled away and stepped back, almost knocking into the shelves. The back room was small, and with him and his dog taking up most of the space, it felt like a coat closet.

He wore camouflage pants, which hugged the stacked muscles of his thighs, a white t-shirt, and an American flag bandana around his neck—a match to the one around the dog's neck. A bunch of tattoos covered his forearms and one wound around an insanely large bicep. Being this close, she got a first hand look at the ink: a Marine Corps logo and a cross in bold red colors.

"Are you Mr. July?"

His forehead creased. "Excuse me?"

She waved the stupid Uncle Sam hat.

He chuckled. "I guess I am, but I don't think that's my style."

That twinkle in his eye caused a flush of heat into her stomach and she almost fanned herself with the hat. A vision of him wearing *just* the hat careened into her mind.

"It's not for you," she said quickly, trying to get a grip and *not* stare at his…everything. "It's for him." Savannah pointed to the mammoth with a glare. The dog whined and sniffed the air before licking his chops. "Why do I feel like his lunch?"

Peed-On Man leaned in and she froze. Oh God, he smelled amazing too? *Figures.* He bent his head close and for a split second she thought he was going to kiss her. Not that she'd mind.

He sniffed and straightened in a flash. "Yup, thought so."

What in the world? "Is there a problem?"

"Peanut butter," he stated with a nod.

"This is so bizarre," she mumbled before she could help herself.

"You smell like peanut butter," he clarified and crossed his arms, causing more bulging of arm muscles. He really needed to stop doing that.

"You say that to all the girls?" Quick wit and comebacks were her specialty. She'd won many a case in court due to being fast on her feet. So his gorgeous self and crazy dog made her lose that ability momentarily, well it was back now. Plus, it helped get her pulse to a normal pace.

He smirked. "You like it? I'll be sure to put it in my repertoire."

"Happy to help in the romance department," she said flippantly. Oddly, the thought of him using a pickup line on some woman made her frown.

Savannah grabbed the American flag off the shelf, fully intending to brush past him and end the conversation.

He placed a hand on her arm. "It's why Sniper pounced."

"Huh?"

"You must have eaten peanut butter. It's his favorite." He dropped his hand and patted the peanut-loving culprit on the head and Sniper whined.

The touch of his fingers on her arm lingered. "Well no more of that, mister," she said to the dog to avoid looking at *him*. "I felt like an ice cream cone." Sniper woofed deep and she couldn't resist patting him on the head. "Oh, all right. You're forgiven."

Peed-On Man hooted. A dimple the size of the Grand Canyon appeared on his left cheek, just underneath that interesting scar.

She tore her attention away from the spot and shot out a hand. "By the way, I'm Savannah Moore." If he wasn't going to introduce himself, she might as well. It was only polite.

He nodded, but didn't take her offer. "I know. Augusta told me where to find you. Said you were going to be super nice to me because of yesterday and all…"

So Augusta *did* know who Peed-On Man was after all. Wonder why she hadn't admitted it? And didn't he know exchanging names was the polite thing to do? "You have me at a disadvantage then."

"Now we're even." He snatched the hat from her with a wink, pulled on Sniper's leash, and walked out, giving her a bird's eye view of his extraordinary back side.

By the time she'd recovered enough to come out of the backroom, he and his dog were with Pete, who was attempting to shove Sniper into a sitting position.

"Didn't Mac find you in the storeroom?" Augusta

asked with a confused look motioning toward Savannah still holding the flag.

"Mac?"

"Marc MacDonald, but everyone calls him Mac." Augusta pointed to *him*. "He said he wanted to thank you for ruining his shirt," Augusta said with a giggle.

"Don't even," she warned her sister. "You knew he'd be here today. Don't try any matchmaking stuff. God, how embarrassing," she muttered.

"You're blushing. Could it be you like him?" Augusta crossed her arms, with a mischievous gleam in her eyes, all proud of herself. "I mean, not that I blame you. He's freaking gorgeous." Augusta grabbed the flag and headed to the area set up for the photo shoot.

Savannah regarded the "freaking gorgeous" man in question and had to agree one hundred percent. He wore combat boots and casually leaned against a stool, Sniper at his feet. Long dark hair was pulled into a ponytail at the back of his muscular neck and he positively oozed testosterone. As Peter snapped photos, Mac smiled like a natural in front of the camera. The tingles still lingered in her hand. Guess he wasn't too mad about his shirt, or he wouldn't have been so…flirty, right?

She usually steered far away from men of his size and strength. Ever since that fateful night when one big thug tried to use her as a pincushion.

But for some odd reason, "Mac" wasn't intimidating at all. Maybe it was his quick grin or the way he handled Sniper. There was a tangible bond between dog and master and Mac's expression softened whenever he looked down at him.

Pete stopped to change the lens on the camera and Mac's gaze found hers. Oh damn, he'd caught her staring.

❄ ❄ ❄

Savannah was staring. And from the adorable blush invading her cheeks, he had the feeling she felt the attraction, too. He knew firsthand about one of Sniper's attacks. Damn dog needed to learn he was no lightweight. But she'd taken it like a champ.

She had a killer body—petite, but with just the right amount of curve to her hips, and small-sized breasts...*phew,* it was getting hot in here. He'd never been much of a boob man, even when Gena insisted having hers "enhanced" for him, on his dime, of course.

"Done here," Pete announced, pulling Mac's mind back. Poor Pete had earned his stripes keeping Sniper posed for the pictures.

Pete held out his hand. "Hey, thanks for hooking my buddy up with the VA. He appreciates the help."

"Glad it worked out." Mac returned the gesture and led Sniper to the bowls of food Augusta provided as a reward for the four-legged guests. A few people stopped to say hello and Mac smiled in acknowledgement.

He'd done zero dating since moving to Havenport— no time, no inclination—but as of yesterday morning, a certain woman had invaded his mind.

Well, then, get your ass in gear, Mac. He shrugged into his leather motorcycle jacket and searched for Savannah. Maybe if he were lucky, he could make her blush again. Except the area behind the register was empty.

Well, shit. Where had she gone?

"Thanks, everyone, for participating. It means the world to me, the animal shelter, and to Wags and Walks." Augusta's voice rang out and people clapped.

He found Sniper still wolfing down food and scanned the crowd for Savannah, but came up empty.

"Thanks a bunch, Mac." Augusta approached with a smile.

"I hope this raises a lot of money for the shelter." Maybe if he stuck around making polite conversation, Savannah might come back.

"Well, it's a two-fold purpose," Augusta explained, "the shelter needs the funds but I'd like to build up business here, too. How do you do it? Seems like your shop is always busy."

He gave her a lopsided grin. "I take care of my client's four wheeled babies. You take care of the four legged ones."

Augusta laughed. "I like that! Not that I'm complaining at all, business has picked up lately. Havenport and the people are good for the soul—for a lot of us, I suspect."

She had a point. The town had a soothing atmosphere, and being around the friendly people who called it home took away some of the anxiety he'd lived with for the past few years since leaving the Corps. "That is true."

A woman with a short, red velvet dress that left little to the imagination waved at him. Did he know her? Dark hair was pulled so tightly against her scalp, he got a headache looking at it.

Trailing behind her was none other than the runt who'd peed on him. "Great," he groaned without thinking better of it.

Augusta cocked an eyebrow. "You and Brutus are well acquainted, huh? Or is it his owner you're interested in?"

His face must have shown his horror, for Augusta covered her laugh with her palm.

"My momma taught me if I didn't have something nice to say—say nothing. No. *She's* not the person I'd like to spend time with." Might as well get it out in the open. Maybe Augusta could help with his efforts for her sister.

"Oh really?" she asked, all innocence. "Hmm...funny, I can't think of many single women in town, besides myself—and no offense—you're not my type."

He grinned like a fool. "None taken." Augusta was drop dead gorgeous, but well, he saw her more as a female friend or pal than a potential anything else. "However, there is someone that comes to my mind. Where did she run off to?"

Augusta's smile faltered. "Savannah had to take a phone call. I'll try to put a good word in for you, okay?"

"I need a good word, huh?" He'd rarely had problems getting a date, but he'd been out of the pool for so long, he must have been off his stride.

Augusta shook her head. "It's not you, Mac, believe me. Tell you what, I'll work on her and keep you posted."

"Sounds good." He whistled for Sniper. Wonder what that hesitation was all about? Either way, he looked forward to getting to know Ms. Savannah Moore.

Rap, rap, rap. Steady pounding infiltrated the delicious dream she fought to hold on to, of strong arms pulling her against a rock hard chest and silky dark hair tickling her cheek...

"Havenport FD. Open up or we'll break down the door!"

Well *that* wasn't what she'd hoped the dream led toward. She snuggled deeper under the covers and willed away the sound.

More pounding and Savannah sat up, disoriented. What was that smell? She coughed into the crook of her arm. Was that a haze floating around the room? Something was burning. *Something is burning?* Holy...

She flung the blankets aside, shot out of bed, and bounded down the hallway. "Wait, I'm coming. Do not break in!" The apartment above Augusta's shop was only temporary, but that didn't mean she could afford to replace anything. The closer she got to the door, the more pungent the smell became—of burnt toast and sulfur.

Savannah undid the chain and flung the door wide open. A blast of cold air hit her like a bucket of ice. She shivered, feeling practically naked in the Boston University tank top and flannel pajama bottoms.

A fireman dressed in full gear filled the threshold.

"Smoke...shop...safe..." His voice was muffled.

"I can't understand you." She pointed to his mask. More firemen stomped around at the bottom of the back stairs leading to her apartment and her heart sank. "Is there a fire?"

What the hell was happening? Had she left the stupid snow maker on? Oh God. Augusta was going to be devastated.

The fireman pulled off his mask and Savannah did a double take. Wait, was she still dreaming? Only this time Mac was dressed as a fireman instead of being half naked.

"Savannah, you have to get out. Smoke's coming from the store below."

His words set in and she rubbed at her arms trying to clear the sleep from her head. God, it was freezing. Then she saw him cringe at the network of crisscrossed scars, which ran across her chest, and from her shoulder to her left elbow. The series of plastic surgeries had helped a lot, but the disfigurement to her bicep was still there and always would be.

She had nothing to be ashamed of. And she'd be damned if she let him look at her with pity.

She lifted her chin a notch and met his stare. "Let me get my coat and boots."

He blinked and cleared his throat. "Of course, but make it quick."

She pivoted on a heel and felt his eyes on her back as she hurried to the closet. Grabbing her parka, she stuffed her feet into boots and hooked her purse over her shoulder on the way out. On the landing, he stepped aside so she could go down the stairs first.

A plume of white smoke billowed into the night sky and she swayed, gripping the ice-cold metal railing. Mac must have noticed her falter for his hand grabbed under her elbow.

"Steady," he said close to her ear, and ushered her down the steps to a point near one of the fire trucks. People began to filter into the street and someone called out a question to Mac, but he didn't answer. The door to Wags and Walks was wide open and the front window was shattered, glass littering the sidewalk. Had the firemen done that damage?

"Augusta…" Her voice came out in a strange whisper. She coughed from the sting of smoke in her throat.

"Drink this." Mac pulled a bottle of water from one of the outside pockets in his fire jacket. "Someone will call her. I have to go and help."

The water wasn't cold, but she didn't care, it was wet and she almost moaned from the relief to her parched throat. How long had she been asleep, breathing those fumes?

His gaze searched her face. "Will you be okay here?"

She nodded and let out a long breath. "Of course. Do what you have to. Please, Mac, Augusta cannot lose the store." Her voice cracked, though she tried like hell to keep it together.

He cupped her chin in one of his big fireproof gloves. "We'll take care of it."

Her heart did a little flip and he walked away.

"Savannah!" Augusta shoved her way through the crowd and hugged her hard. "This is crazy. Are you okay?"

"I'm fine. I'm so sorry. If I left that stupid snow machine on then this is all my fault." How in the world was she going to make up for wrecking the shop? She shivered just thinking about the outcome.

Augusta frowned. "Of course it's not your fault. I checked everything before I locked up." Augusta rubbed her hands together and blew breath into them. It had to be well after midnight and getting colder by the minute. The lights from the fire truck flashed and Savannah surveyed the crowd for Mac.

"Close up your jacket, Savvy. You'll get sick."

She pulled her jacket close and turned to Augusta. "Mac came to get me. You didn't tell me he was a fireman." Their conversation after the photo shoot covered the general bases—Mac's garage, his being a former Marine, and also single—something Augusta made it a point to relay loud and clear.

"He's a volunteer," Augusta stated. "My heart nearly stopped when I drove up and saw all the smoke. I thought…after all you went through…well you don't want to know." Augusta wrung her hands and shivered.

She reached for Augusta's hands and gave them a squeeze. "How did you know to come?" Augusta lived on the outskirts of town in a tiny home she shared with a menagerie of pets. Savannah loved animals, but she wasn't about to sleep with a zoo of them.

"The alarm company called and said the alarm had tripped, that's when I came right away. I wish I knew what was going on." Her expression was grave. Hell, Augusta's life savings was sunk into Wags and Walks.

Finally one of the firemen came out of the store and

asked people to back up. "Folks," he said above the crowd's voices, "nothing to see. The smoke is contained and all is safe. Please go back to your nice warm homes."

Where was Mac? She hadn't seen him since he'd left her at least twenty minutes ago.

"Time to find out what's up." Augusta started for the fireman.

Mac's voice called out and they both turned. *Please let him have positive news.*

"The store isn't bad, it was only smoke," he said in answer to Augusta's questions.

Her lawyer's sixth sense shot into overdrive. Only smoke? He wasn't telling the whole story. His fists were clenched and he seemed tense perusing the crowd. Was he searching for something or some*one* maybe?

"There wasn't any fire?" she asked.

He stopped his crowd searching and met her gaze. "Someone threw a smoke grenade through the store window."

"Who would do such a thing?" Augusta's voice rose and a few lingering bystanders shot her glances.

Savannah's stomach sank. *And why?* Havenport wasn't exactly the crime capital of the world. The rate was practically nil with the exception of a DUI or two because of the bar in town. She knew the crime stats, had somewhat of a compulsion for researching them. Plus, she'd thoroughly investigated Havenport before Augusta settled here.

"Maybe it was some kind of prank." She hoped so.

His lips flattened. "You both need to come inside and I'll show you."

She frowned. "Show us what? Did some college kids do something stupid?"

School *was* out for the holidays, so maybe. But still, Mac was being awfully cryptic.

"Tell us what's going on," she demanded.

"Savannah, calm down." Augusta grabbed her arm, stopping her forward motion. She hadn't realized she'd practically lunged at Mac. Her pulse beat steady in her ear like a marching band inside her head, and made her feel dizzy. Maybe it was the smoke, but more than likely, it was a wave like she hadn't felt in long time bubbling up again. *Get control.*

Augusta was right. A few cleansing breaths helped.

"Show us," she finally said to Mac, and he nodded tightly before heading toward the open doorway. Filing behind Augusta into the store, she looked around and wanted to cry. They'd have to vacuum every inch of the place twenty times over to make sure none of the dogs got glass in their paws. It was everywhere. Her boots crunched as Mac lead them to the far end of the store, where the grooming tables were set up.

Mac grabbed a plastic bag off the table and held it up to them.

"This smoke grenade isn't anything special," he explained. "Could've been bought anywhere, even home made."

"Maybe Savannah was right then, and it's just a bunch of drunk kids out for a cheap thrill?" Augusta speculated.

Mac reached back and retrieved another bag from the table, this one sealed. There was a white piece of paper inside. "I think it's more than that. The police want to investigate."

The words written on the paper made her blood icy: "*You testify, you die.*" Her knees turned into jelly and white spots appeared in her vision.

❄ ❄ ❄

"Mac, quick, she's going to fall." Augusta grabbed for Savannah, but he'd noticed her swaying and snapped into action, catching her slight frame before she crumbled to the floor. Her face had lost all its color and Augusta moaned her sister's name again, clutching at his arm.

"I've got her." Gently, he hoisted Savannah onto the grooming table. She barely weighed anything, but she was limp, and her shallow breathing worried him. Had she succumbed to smoke inhalation? He'd seen a few people suffer the after effects since working for the Havenport FD. Her apartment *was* hazy, but nothing compared to the store below before the smoke had cleared.

Something twitched in his gut and hairs stood at the back of his neck. He'd felt the same sensation in combat, just when shit was about to hit the fan.

That note. It was no neighborhood prank.

And if those scars on Savannah were what he suspected, she'd been attacked. "I need a bus ASAP," he turned his head, speaking into his radio.

Mere minutes passed before the ambulance arrived. Savannah stirred as the EMTs hoisted her onto a gurney.

"What's going on?" she asked, groggy. The paleness of her skin made the blue depths of her eyes more vibrant.

"I think the smoke got to you," Augusta piped in, looking worried.

Deep in his gut, he knew Savannah's reaction wasn't only from the smoke.

Something was up—something scary enough to make her faint.

"I'll follow the ambulance." Mac said, grabbing his fireproof gloves off the table.

Mac caught the quick negative shake Savannah gave to Augusta and a strange expression pass between the sisters.

"It's okay, Mac. I'll be with her. I'm sure you're needed here."

Hearing the words, Savannah seemed to relax and her head fell back onto the pillow as she was wheeled away. Something didn't add up and he wanted answers.

❄ ❄ ❄

Music filtered through the air the closer she came to Mac's shop. Savannah had sprung herself out of the ER earlier in the morning, and, after a good long nap at Augusta's place she was ready to tackle the day.

And Mac deserved an explanation too.

Moores did not back down.

She hadn't undergone hours of surgery and the pain of rehabilitation to back down now. She *would* testify. Neither a threatening note, nor smoke bomb was going to change that. The January 2nd trial couldn't come fast enough. Havenport PD understood the situation and had agreed to keep an extra officer on duty just in case there was more trouble. She hoped not.

Guess trying to escape to the peace and quiet of Havenport had backfired. Luckily she still had a few friends in the Chicago FBI office. For the time being Augusta was protected—whether she liked it or not—and she was never going to figure out the agent assigned to her detail until the trial finished.

The least she could give back to Augusta for all her support these past few months.

One of the glass garage doors was open with a foreign car parked inside. Probably cost more than she made in the DA's office in one year—or *had* made. No use thinking about her shrinking bank account. Once the trial finished, she had some decisions to make about her future.

First things first.

Mac's head was under the hood of a tiny sports car and she felt no shame in ogling his jeans, which fit him like a glove and were faded in all the right places. She knocked on the side of the wall. "Hello? Mac?"

He straightened and his eyes widened. "Hey," he said over the blaring music, then held up his hand and moved to his workbench. The music stopped and he was at her side in a minute.

"How are you?" he asked and scanned her up and down fixedly. Savannah had the feeling not much got past him. At least this morning her scars were covered in layers of sweater and bulky coat, but he must remember them.

Might as well just get to it. "I came to apologize for doing an imitation of a sack of potatoes on you." The words came out in a rush.

He regarded her without speaking.

"I can't thank you enough for being so cool and in control about the whole incident. I used to be that way too." She sighed heavily. "I'm trying to be that way…again."

Now why had she blurted that? Not only had her sense of confidence left, but he probably thought she was a loon.

"Well thanks again, you seem really busy." Rocky Road could make her forget this conversation ever happened. She pivoted on her heel and headed back toward the door.

"Savannah, wait," he urged, and she turned around.

"The police were here earlier."

Her stomach sank. *Uh oh.* Time for that explanation.

"Mac…I—"

"Let me clean up first and then we'll talk?" His voice went up, as if in a question, while he wiped his hands on a rag, then disappeared into a small bathroom before she could respond.

The garage was pristine, from the floor mats below the car lifts to the gleaming metal tools hanging on pegboards. The car he'd been working on was a two-seater convertible. She leaned in close for a look at the hood ornament: Maserati. *Nice.*

"Okay, I'm all done." He'd put on a clean white tee that fit him like a second skin, and revealed a hint of chest hair—dark and curly—showing above the collar. "You want to grab some lunch maybe? I'm starving."

No sign of pity lingered in his eyes like it had yesterday.

"Sure."

"I'll tell Carol so she knows." He grabbed a leather jacket off the coat rack and disappeared into the reception area.

"There's a great pizza place around the corner," he stated when he returned.

"Lead the way." She'd thought long and hard last night on what to tell him if he asked. She liked Mac, so why not just be honest? She was so tired of trying to put on a sophisticated lawyer persona. Since hanging up her black suit, although not of her doing, she felt lighter somehow. Events had changed her outlook on many things, and if being attacked had taught her anything, it was that life was meant to live.

Inside the shop, the smells of tomato sauce and fresh dough hit her nose and a loud growl came from her stomach. "Guess I'm starving, too."

He chuckled.

They found a table, and the waitress took their order.

Mac's gaze scouted the place front to back, like he was scoping a crime scene.

"You remind me of the police detectives I used to deal with."

His attention snapped back to her. "You were PD?"

She shook her head. "God, no. I was with the State's Attorney's office in Cook County, Chicago until…I left almost a year ago."

"Because of your arm?" he asked and she inhaled sharply. Of course he'd have questions about that.

"Yes. One of the perps, a gang member I was prosecuting didn't like the idea of spending the rest of his life behind bars. Guess he thought slashing his girlfriend and leaving her for dead didn't warrant jail time." She laughed tightly. Back then, she could never have been flippant about such things.

His jaw clenched. "What happened?"

"Well, he posted bail—which was *not* my recommendation—but his attorney won that argument. One night he was hiding by my car in the parking garage." She shivered although the pizza shop was rather warm. "I was lucky, the security guard found me. Guess it wasn't my time." She'd done her fair share of thanking God a million ways to Sunday for that, too.

He rubbed the back of his neck and let out a cynical laugh. "I know all about that sentiment," he said, pointing to his scar. "Sniper bullet grazed me, happened in the sandbox last tour. An inch more and I would've been shipped home in a box. You start to think about your own mortality after something like that."

"I'd wondered," she stammered, "about that scar, I mean, when I first met…or when Brutus did his thing." Oh God, there went her blush again at his grin.

He reached over the table to envelop her hands in his warm ones. "Please." He groaned with a smirk. "Let's not talk about that mutt." His smile faded. "Your reaction to that note had something to do with the attack, correct?"

She swallowed hard and nodded. "I took a leave of absence after it happened. Now, it seems someone on the outside, considering *he's* currently incarcerated, does not want me to testify at the trial next month." Admitting the truth out loud hit home just how messed up the situation had become.

Mac was awfully easy to talk to, and his physical and mental strength made it easy to lean on him for support, but that didn't mean her problems were his.

He frowned and squeezed her hands. "The police are worried the vandalism to the shop could escalate into something dangerous for you. I am, too.

She pulled away and straightened her ponytail. "I'm aware of how the local police feel. Look, I'm really sorry to dump all this on you." *Way to scare away a gorgeous guy.* "I only wanted to thank you for last night."

He regarded her in silence, and she got lost in his green depths. His demeanor was deadly calm, but his face told a different story—like he was coiled and ready for anything. It was a little scary and a lot sexy at the same time.

He leaned forward and reached for her hand, running his fingertips on her palm before squeezing it gently. "I promise you. As long as you are in this town, if someone dares to touch you again, they'll have to deal with me."

His words made her stomach flutter. Fortunately the pizza arrived at that exact moment.

❊ ❊ ❊

Mac was all for being strong and a woman taking care of herself, but in Savannah's case, her situation was crazy dangerous. He'd seen his share of ex gang members in the Corps. Kids that'd been under his command who'd cleaned up their acts at boot camp—but their stories were violent.

If someone didn't want Savannah to testify, then her attorney, or the prosecutor's office, or *someone* had better protect her. But how could he make her understand that?

"I've been around some pretty hardnosed guys in the Corps. This smoke grenade was a warning. Maybe it's something you should consider heeding."

She took a bite of her pizza and flashed him a heated look. "You sound like Augusta. I'm not afraid, nor will I back down."

"This is not about backing down at all. Tell you what, if you won't listen to me, how about you learn from me?"

Her eyebrows creased. "How?"

"I'll teach you how to defend yourself. I used to be an instructor." She was small, but with the correct training she could take down a mountain.

She dropped the pizza onto her plate. "You mean fight? I took a self-defense course back in law school."

He arched an eyebrow. "How'd that work against a knife attack? Or what if that smoke grenade turns into someone coming after you again?"

She opened and closed her mouth before her lips compressed. "What do you have in mind?"

There it was—the spark he wanted to see. "Meet me at the garage after five and wear comfortable clothes."

She tilted her head and regarded him. "If this is your idea of asking me on a date, it needs work."

He gave her a lazy grin. Oh she wanted a date huh? "Safety first, then we'll have that date…you can count on it."

There went that adorable blush again.

At five sharp Savannah waited for him inside the reception area, talking to Carol. Her hair was in a ponytail and her oversized BU hoodie covered running pants. Tight running pants. Oh boy, teaching young marines the basics of martial arts was one thing. Teaching a sexy woman was quite another.

"Have fun you two." Carol winked at him.

Carol and Savannah shared a smile and he felt like the odd man out. "You and Carol are chummy," he noted.

"She's funny. Reminds me of my Gran. So where to?" she asked.

"I have a gym in my house. It's not far if you don't mind walking?" His rent included use of a smaller building. It needed work, but so far he'd installed a variety of gym equipment from his old place, including the ramp.

"It's around the back." He let Sniper out of the main house before leading Savannah to the detached building, which used to be a cottage house. Sniper went in first and headed to his huge dog bed in the corner.

"Wow, this place is great." She took in the equipment and touched the punching bag suspended from the ceiling. "What's the ramp for?"

"When I lived in California, guys came back from war pretty banged up," he explained. "So I converted my garage where they could rehab at their own pace and stay free of charge. My plan is to help local vets once I convince the owner to sell me this place."

She punched the bag a few times with control. It was a bit of a reach, but she had a good southpaw for a little thing. The only sound between them was its ticking. Would she think his efforts were stupid, like Gena had?

"Why did you move?" she asked finally.

He shrugged, almost snorting. "Life changed." No use getting into the Gena fiasco.

There was surprise and something else in her expression. Something which triggered a twitching low on his spine.

"You're an exceptional man, Marc MacDonald."

Whoa. How could he possibly respond to *that?*

Savannah approached the weight bench where he sat, and straddled it. He forced back a gulp. He could have slapped himself for staying mute. She touched his hand lightly and gave him a slight smile that punched him in the gut and left no mercy.

"I became immune to people doing good things after prosecuting so many *bad* people—until I came here. Havenport's wonderful. The people are special. They care for the sake of caring. It was kind of disconcerting at first." A blush stole into her cheeks and she glanced down at the bench. "What you want to do for the vets—that makes you special, too. Underneath all that rock hard muscle."

Well, hell. Unexpected warmth invaded his chest. It was nice to be thought of in a good way for a change instead of as a cold-hearted bastard. He cleared his throat, cutting through the blanket of silence. "You ready to get started?"

She chewed on her lips, and he almost groaned. The bottom one was plump and his base instincts shouted to try a taste. He unzipped his jacket to give his hands something to do besides reach across the bench for her. Thankfully, the Marine Corps tank he'd put on at the garage was lightweight. His body was overheating like a faulty engine.

Her gaze traveled down his torso. She cleared her throat too.

Oh, this was going to be interesting.

She crossed her arms, grasping the bottom of the hoodie, pulled it over her head, and revealed a white tank top. Her arms were small, muscles defined, with the exception of her left bicep. It was caved in at a point above her elbow.

The roadmap of scars, and the flash of determination in her gaze when he raised his to meet hers cut into his psyche.

No one was ever going to hurt Savannah again.

Whoa, where had these protective instincts come from? He'd never felt an iota of this emotion in all three years with Gena.

Savannah lifted her chin, challenging him to say something.

"Bring it on, sensei."

He stood and with legs apart, assumed a combat stance. "We'll start with the basics. An attacker is coming at you, say, in an alley or parking garage."

She chuckled. "Honestly?" She snorted. "You think I'm going to be alone in an alley or garage again?"

His breath came out in a huff. "Work with me, Moore. First, strike at the throat." He brought his forearm chin level to show her the move. "Bring force up and into it. Use your body weight, no matter how slight it is," he muttered.

She rose and moved closer to him. An alluring scent hit his nose—a mix of peaches and musk. God, it was sexier than anything he'd ever experienced.

"Pfft...sorry. I'm not Mike Tyson, *MacDonald,"* came another wisecrack but the underlying tone was shaky. It was obvious she was nervous. Perhaps his words earlier had hit home, or maybe she was as affected by their closeness as he was.

"A blow to the throat will cause momentary asphyxiation, disarming your attacker so he's stunned and his torso will bend out, like this." He stuck out his chest and it grazed hers. She gasped then swallowed. He was close enough to see her throat muscles move.

"Jab straight to the solar plexus." He pointed to his stomach. "The attacker will bend forward from the blow. Then step in and knee the groin."

An eyebrow arched and her lips parted. "The groin, huh?"

He ignored the question, mainly because his groin area had chosen to misbehave when she licked her lips. *Christ.* "You want to try it?"

She backed up and nodded.

He rolled his shoulders. *Keep it together, Mac.*

"Should I pretend to be texting?" There was no sarcasm in the request. Maybe she was taking this seriously after all.

"Whatever scenario works."

She walked across the room, giving him a view of her shapely behind in those tight pants and his fists clenched. He imagined filling his hands with…time to shut down caveman mode.

"Ready?" She smirked, as if knowing he'd been ogling her backside.

"Come here," he said, his voice coming out husky.

She pretended to be engrossed in her invisible phone and he approached in predatory mode that had more to do with his baser instincts than a self-defense lesson. Using his size, he sought to dominate her space. He moved close and wrapped a hand around her tiny wrist as she tried to pass.

Without hesitating she bashed him in the Adams apple. He grunted at the force of her fist striking his ribs then she stepped between his legs and raised a knee—but stopped.

They were close enough that he saw the length of her lashes. His heart thumped in his chest. A drop of sweat ran from the indent of her throat, disappearing under the edge of her collar.

"Do I get an 'A' from the teacher?" Her breath hit his lips and a bolt of desire slammed into him. Excitement, wanting…hell, it was worse than an explosion in the heat of combat, and he reacted on instinct.

※ ※ ※

Yes! *Finally.* Mac's lips found hers and a dam broke inside—one that had been buried and feared dead since the attack. God, to have this awesome, strong, considerate, caring man want to help her, touched every feminine atom in her body. She wound her arms around his strong shoulders and got up on her tiptoes, barely scratching the surface of how up close and personal she wanted to get to him.

He reached under her butt and hauled her up, winding her legs around his waist. She moaned into his open mouth. The feel of his hands burned through the thin material of her leggings. He strode forward and she held on for dear life as her back hit the wall. He pushed into her and every single inch of him seared against her. *Freaking amazing.*

He nibbled on the corner of her mouth. "Jesus, Savannah, I'm going to incinerate here."

"Not on your life." She wrapped her arms around his head and pulled off the rubber band holding his hair. It was just as silky as in her dream. He opened her mouth wider for the delicious attack of his tongue against hers.

Woof, woof, growl. Sniper chose that moment to interrupt.

Mac pulled an inch away from her and pierced her with his intense gaze.

A peek around his shoulders showed Sniper scratching at the door.

He bent his forehead against hers and let out a frustrated groan. "Big guy needs to go out." His chest heaved, a steady thump under her palm.

"He's got great timing, huh?" She chuckled against his lips and he growled too, at the same time her stomach did.

"You cannot be hungry," he said incredulous.

He slowly released her legs and she slid down his body with a smirk. "Got any ice cream?" It would certainly help cool down every inch of her sizzling body.

He let out a shaky laugh, shook his head, and gave her a quick peck. "I'll let him out and take a look in my freezer."

Mac returned a few minutes later without Sniper, but carrying a pint of Ben and Jerry's. *Score*. Suddenly, uncertainty hit. Their kiss was amazing, her lips still tingled from the intensity, but this was crazy.

Havenport was only supposed to be a temporary thing and she wasn't sure if getting involved with Mac was good for her head at this time.

"You're thinking too much." He put the pint on the bench, took her hands between his large ones, and smiled down at her.

"Listen, Mac…"

His perfect lips flattened and a vee formed in his forehead. "Those words are usually followed by get out, or you've fucked up my brand new car," he joked.

She couldn't help laughing. "Considering I'm in your place and my car is a '05 Toyota; the chances of that are slim and none."

He ran his knuckles lightly down her cheek and she wanted to sink into his touch. "What then?"

She swallowed, trying to pick her words carefully.

"My life is complicated now. The upcoming trial…it's going to get intense and I'll be gone from town for months, maybe. As much as I want to jump into—" She hesitated a beat. "Well, you could probably guess where I want to be *jumping*."

He stopped the rest of her tirade with his finger against her lips. "That was amazing, but I didn't bring you to my home for that purpose, and I feel like a jerk."

Could he possibly be for real? A guy apologizing for making her want to do so many delicious things to… "I was into it too, so do not apologize, *MacDonald*. But seriously, if someone is after me, the last thing I want is for anyone else to get hurt. It's bad enough Augusta's store was trashed."

"You think I give a shit about getting hurt? Hell, I've been to war." He cupped the back of her head and tilted it back so she was forced meet his gaze. It was the most erotic gesture she'd ever experienced.

"Whatever this *thing* is between us, it's quick and hot and better than anything I've had—which blows me away probably more than you know. So wherever it's headed or not, let's just see what happens, okay?" His eyes implored her with an uncertainty, which was surprising, given his warrior-like persona.

But he made sense. Why not just enjoy him? For the first time in a long while, something felt right. He was so damned attractive and that kiss still left her breathless. "I don't even know if Havenport is someplace I want to stay. I *will* have to work again."

"Don't make this complicated," he told her. "If I've learned anything from relocating and rebuilding my life, it's to take one day at a time."

She'd uttered the same thing to herself many times.

"And if you're willing, I'd like to spend as many of those days with you as possible. Fair enough?"

Savannah wanted to throw caution to the wind and jump back into his arms. But could she? One last-ditch argument inside her head—like the good lawyer in her—to convince herself to walk away wasn't working.

"Fair enough."

His kiss to her nose sent pulses of warmth into her heart. "I brought two spoons, but I have a feeling I'm not getting any ice cream, am I?"

"Not unless you have your own pint." She chuckled.

The holidays were going to be better than she expected.

❄ ❄ ❄

"You *said* you'd spend the next few days doing anything I wanted, so no complaining, MacDonald," she scolded him as they waited in line outside The Final Chapter for the book signing. There was a nice sized crowd of people anticipating meeting someone named Beth Alexander, and JD Watson as well as her favorite, Winnie.

Mac pulled her close against his side and assessed the crowd. "*All* these people read romance?" Most of the crowd consisted of women, but there was a smattering of men in the line.

Since it was Sunday, Mac's garage was closed, so they had all day to spend together and she couldn't be happier. In the short time she'd gotten to know more about him, she felt this amazing connection. Sure, he was sexy as anything, and kissing him made her want to swoon. But it was more than that. Mac had a way of making her feel more confident about herself—a feeling she'd lost. She'd sure need confidence for what lay ahead next month.

The glass for Wags and Walks was scheduled for installation tomorrow, and yesterday after their "lesson," and much more kissing—her face warmed at the memory—Mac had helped Augusta clean the shop from top to bottom.

They stepped inside the bookstore and the owner waved, recognizing Mac. "You shop here?"

He feigned an insulted look. "I do know how to read."

She punched him in the chest and had to rub her knuckles. God, he was solid. "And here my first impression of you and your wet shirt was more brawn than brains."

"Very funny counselor," he teased and grabbed her around the stomach to tickle her side.

She laughed and tried to squirm out of his embrace. "Stop that. People are staring." April stood at the other end of the table, glaring. "I think someone is jealous," Savannah whispered out the side of her mouth.

Mac glanced to where she'd tipped her head and winced. "Now I recognize her. She's been coming to the garage every week for some non-existent car problems."

"At least her dog got to know you," she teased.

"Yeah, don't remind me."

They finally made it to the table where Winnie sat. Savannah gushed for a few fan girl minutes telling Winnie how much she loved her work. Mac squeezed her hand gently then excused himself with a slightly embarrassed grin as Winnie discussed the cover model.

After paying for the signed copy, she found Mac standing by the Christmas tree. His sharp gaze scoped the entire store. She felt more protected now than those first weeks after the attack when a police detail had practically stood at her door every day.

Mac's concern was genuine, not just a duty, like he'd stop anything or anyone who came at her.

Something in her heart shifted. She placed her hand in his. "Can I ask you a favor?"

His eyebrows rose. "Anything," he answered. No hesitation.

"Will you spend Christmas with me and Augusta?"

His face split into a wide grin. "That's not a favor, that's a pleasure. You might have to fight Carol for me, though."

She winked. "Oh don't worry, we've worked it out."

He laughed. "What am I, a piece of meat? Don't answer that," he said quickly while he fixed her scarf around her neck.

It was little gestures he did for her without thought, like this, just on pure instinct, which made her feel protected and treasured somehow. It was weird and exciting.

Her favorite Bing Crosby song played on the shop's sound system and they stepped outside to falling snow. "Looks like it might be a white Christmas after all, hmm?"

Mac's breath came out in frosty puffs and flakes clung to his lashes. He glanced up at the sky. "This one's going to be big, according to the reports. Come stay with me tonight. I'd feel better just in case...I don't know. I'll take the couch."

Was that a blush on *his* cheeks? Whether he was embarrassed or not the protectiveness and chivalry made her heart sing. "I'll need to get a few things and check in with Augusta. Why don't you go home, take care of Sniper, and then come by the apartment in an hour?"

"Sure thing. I'll call your cell before I come to get you." He gave her a quick peck before she turned and headed for Wags and Walks.

❄ ❄ ❄

Savannah's cell went straight to voicemail. Again. The hairs on the back of his neck stood on end as he rounded the corner toward her place. Snow fell in large clumps and didn't help visibility. Why hadn't he gone with her? Sniper whined at his side, loving the snow, yet sensing his upset. "What's going on, pal?" He broke into a sprint through the snow, with Sniper alongside.

The door to her apartment was wide open. Dread seeped into his throat. "Savannah!" Visions of her hurt, attacked, or worse careened into his mind. He was going to kill whoever dared.

Sniper bound up the slippery stairs, Mac on his heels. Then a growl sounded as the dog disappeared into the apartment.

Mac stopped short in the middle of her living room. A man in a ski mask sprawled on the floor—seemingly out cold. Sniper clamped down on a pant leg, and the guy tried to roll over. That is, until he took one look at the mammoth dog and yelped like a girl.

Mac searched the room for Savannah and found her sitting on the floor in the corner. His gut unclenched.

White-hot anger rose into his head and he almost turned back to deliver another blow to the dirt bag on the floor. Sniper must have sensed his rage for he growled and flashed his teeth.

The shoulder of Savannah's shirt was torn, and the corner of her mouth bled. She cradled her fist against her stomach and rocked back and forth, clearly in pain.

"Mac?" She seemed confused, and his heart lodged in his throat.

He knelt. "I'm here," he said gently, trying to control his rage.

"I got him good," she said in a wobbly voice. "Right in the balls, sensei."

He let out a shaky laugh. "That's my girl."

She'd called the police, thankfully, after rendering the guy immobile, and as soon as they arrived, Mac called off Sniper. The officers carted the piece of garbage out and Mac promised he'd bring Savannah to the station to give a statement after she was checked out at the hospital.

He hugged her tight against his chest and pressed his lips to the top of her head. The rush of adrenaline started to subside and he relaxed his grip. She sighed and snuggled closer, snaking her arms around his torso.

"You okay?" His voice was hoarse with emotion.

She looked at him and smiled. "I am now." She bit her lip. "Will you come with me next month to the trial? I could use a strong set of shoulders and a martial arts instructor in my corner. Or…is it too much to ask?"

"You can count on it. And I'm not letting you out of my sight until then."

"For how long?" She gave him a sexy smile.

"How high can you count?" He bent and captured her lips.

About the Author

NICOLE S. PATRICK has always loved to read, and in her teenage years, she "borrowed" her mom's books to sneak away and become lost in the world of romance. After more than ten years in the corporate world of tech recruiting and HR management, she decided to stay home and raise children. But with so many romantic stories and characters floating around in her head, when the kids napped, she was compelled to put those words on a page and pursue this crazy dream of becoming published. Nicole writes romantic suspense and her heroes are those alpha males in uniform. She lives in New Jersey with her real-life hero, her husband, and her two sons.

❅ ❅ ❅

For more information about Nicole, please visit her website at www.NicoleSPatrick.com

Also by Nicole S. Patrick

❄ ❄ ❄

<u>Timeless Tales – Short Stories</u>

Letter From St. Nick featured in Timeless Keepsakes

Poseidon's Strength featured in Timeless Escapes

The Colors of Courage featured in Timeless Treasures

From This Day Forward featured in Timeless Vows

❄ ❄ ❄

<u>Havenport – Novellas</u>

Hometown Hero featured in Welcome to Havenport

A Spirit's Bond featured in Haunted Havenport

Snowbound in Havenport — Fall, 2017

❄ ❄ ❄

We hope you enjoyed your time in Havenport, Rhode Island. If you're like us, and didn't want to leave our small town, we have great news!

Havenport is having a July fourth celebration and you're invited. Revisit old friends and meet some new in **Welcome to Havenport**.

If you're not afraid of ghosts, visit Havenport for Halloween. You'll be sure to run into one or two friendly spirits at the annual Halloween ball in **Haunted Havenport**.

❄ ❄ ❄

If you enjoyed your time in Havenport, please spread the word by leaving a review on the site where you purchased your copy or on a reader site such as Goodreads or Shelfari. Thank you!

❄ ❄ ❄

To receive up-to-date information on future Timeless Scribes publications, please sign up for our mailing list at www.TimelessScribes.com.

Timeless Scribes
Publishing